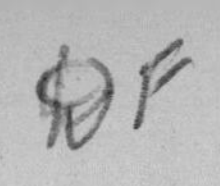

# DOUBLE SHOT!

Clint and Kate were coming out of the dining room when Clint saw Bly coming down the steps. Bly saw him at the same time and surprised Clint by going for his gun.

Clint's quick reaction, despite his surprise, saved his life—and possibly Kate's. With his left hand he pushed her out of the line of fire, while he drew his gun with his right. Bly cleared leather but never got a chance to bring the gun up. Clint shot him in the chest twice. The man tumbled down the steps and was dead before he hit the lobby floor. . . .

**DON'T MISS THESE**
**ALL-ACTION WESTERN SERIES**
**FROM THE BERKLEY PUBLISHING GROUP**

***THE GUNSMITH by J. R. Roberts***
Clint Adams was a legend among lawmen, outlaws, and ladies. They called him . . . the Gunsmith.

***LONGARM by Tabor Evans***
The popular long-running series about U.S. Deputy Marshal Long—his life, his loves, his fight for justice.

***SLOCUM by Jake Logan***
Today's longest-running action Western. John Slocum rides a deadly trail of hot blood and cold steel.

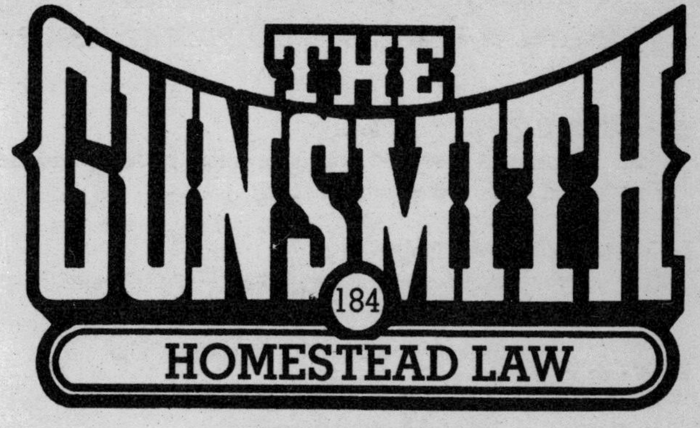


J. R. ROBERTS

J

JOVE BOOKS, NEW YORK

HOMESTEAD LAW

A Jove Book / published by arrangement with the author

PRINTING HISTORY
Jove edition / April 1997



The Putnam Berkley World Wide Web site address is
http://www.berkley.com/berkley

ISBN: 0-515-12051-0

A JOVE BOOK®
Jove Books are published by The Berkley Publishing Group, 200 Madison Avenue, New York, New York 10016.
JOVE and the "J" design are trademarks belonging to Jove Publications, Inc.

PRINTED IN THE UNITED STATES OF AMERICA

10 9 8 7 6 5 4 3 2 1

THE
GUNSMITH
184
HOMESTEAD LAW

# ONE

At the sound of the first shot, Clint Adams hung his head and said, "Shit." He was annoyed because he knew he couldn't ignore what he'd heard. He just wasn't built that way. The shot meant that someone might be in trouble, and in need of help.

"Let's go," Clint said to his black gelding, Duke.

He picked a rise and decided that the shot had come from behind it. When the second shot sounded, followed by a third, he knew he was heading in the right direction.

He rode up the rise and when he got to the top he stopped. On the other side he saw one man pinned down by four or five others. The lone man had a buckboard, and had taken cover behind it. His horse was fidgeting nervously, and Clint thought that if the horse took off on a run the man would be exposed, and as good as dead. He didn't know the circumstances of what was happening down there, but what he could see was five against one, and he never did like those odds.

He decided to simply ride toward the action, fire a few warning shots, and see if he could scare the attackers away without hurting anyone.

"Let's give it a try, Duke."

He gave the big gelding a little kick in the ribs that set him off down the hill at a gallop. Clint drew his gun from his holster and fired a couple of shots in the general direction of the attackers.

The five men had remained on their horses and were firing at the lone man with rifles. The man was firing back, but ineffectively. Clint knew that if he didn't scare them off they'd turn toward him and fire and he'd be in danger. He'd either have to take cover, or pull his own rifle and do some damage.

Luckily the five men must have only been prepared to face one man, because the appearance of a second dissuaded them from their course of action. Clint heard one of them shout, "Let's get out of here!" and they all turned their horses and rode off.

Clint continued to ride, but changed direction so that he was riding toward the buckboard. As he approached it the man stepped out from behind the buckboard with his gun extended. Clint hastily holstered his gun and showed his empty hands.

"Hold on!" he called out. "I just scared those fellows off."

"Yeah, you did," the man said, "but I thought it mighta been 'cause you want to kill me yourself."

"Why would I want to do that?" Clint asked.

The man holstered his gun awkwardly, showing that he wasn't used to wearing one.

"Seems like everybody wants to kill me these

days," the man said, "and all 'cause I'm doin' my job."

"Which is?"

"My name's Simon Butcher," the man said, "and I'm a homestead inspector."

Clint dismounted.

"Which means you do what, exactly?"

"At tax time I inspect people's homes to determine how much tax they have to pay," the man said. "Some people call me a window inspector."

"And why's that?"

"Because windows are a sign of prosperity," the man said.

"You tax people according to how many windows they have?" Clint asked.

"That's one way," the man said, "but it works both ways."

"How so?"

"Sometimes people can get loans according to how many windows they have."

"I see."

"I want to thank you for helping me," Butcher said, stepping forward and extending his hand. "Also, for not wanting to kill me."

Clint shook the man's hand and said, "I'm just glad I was able to help."

"It's not gonna make you very popular around these parts."

They were in Nelson County, in Missouri, near the town of Truxton.

"Did you know any of those men?" Clint asked.

"Probably," Butcher said, "but I didn't get a good enough look to tell. You don't live around here, do you?"

"No," Clint said, "I'm just here visiting a friend."

"Who's your friend?"

"Wiley Wilcox? He has a spread just north of Truxton. Do you know him?"

"Not yet," Butcher said, "but I will. I have to go out to his place eventually. He'll probably want to kill me, too."

Clint studied the man in front of him. He was stockily built, in his thirties, soft-looking, obviously not a man used to defending himself.

"Why do so many people want to kill you, Mr. Butcher?" Clint asked.

"Well," Butcher said, "sometimes my inspections cost them money. Sometimes their taxes end up so high they lose their home, or their business." Butcher shook his head. "Not my fault. I'm just doing my job. I gotta check my horse, Mr. Adams. I hope he wasn't hit."

Clint walked over to the horse with Butcher. The animal was still spooked, but he appeared unhurt.

"Better let him calm down before you try to drive him," Clint said. "There's a lot of white showing in his eyes."

"Yes, you're right," Butcher said. "I'll just wait here a little while for him to calm down."

"I can wait with you, if you like," Clint said, "in case they come back."

"I don't think they'll be back, Mr. Adams, but I appreciate the offer."

"Well," Clint said, "just to be on the safe side, you better reload your gun."

"Oh, yes," Butcher said, "of course."

They both reloaded their weapons, Clint quickly

and deftly, Butcher awkwardly. When that was done Clint climbed up onto Duke's back and looked down at the man.

"Will you be in Truxton at all?" Butcher asked.

"I'll most likely be staying in a hotel there."

"Then I'd like to buy you a drink eventually," Butcher said, "that is, if you'll drink with me in public."

"I will," Clint said. "Sometime this evening?"

"I will find you, Mr. Adams," Butcher said. "I'm very grateful to you."

"When you find me," Clint said, "call me Clint. Okay?"

"If you will call me Simon."

"Simon, it is," Clint said. "I'll see you later for that drink."

Clint turned Duke and headed him toward the town of Truxton. It was the same direction the gunmen had gone.

# TWO

Truxton had two hotels and Clint simply picked the closest one to the livery. He got himself a room, stared longingly at the bed, but couldn't bring himself to go to sleep in the middle of the afternoon, no matter how bone-tired his body felt. He decided to take care of his other need: food.

He took to the streets of Truxton in search of a likely restaurant. The town was small, but seemed prosperous and busy. There were no abandoned buildings, and the streets were busy. Several of the buildings, though, had an odd absence of windows—that is, glass windows. The holes were in the walls for them, but the windows were missing, for whatever reasons.

On a side street he found a small café that looked good. In his experience the small places couldn't afford money for looks, but the food was usually good. He found that to be true with this one, called simply Sally's.

Sally turned out to be a woman in her fifties, thickly built, with a great booming laugh she used to ingratiate herself with her customers.

"How's that steak, honey?" she asked Clint, stopping by his table.

"It's perfect, Sally. Thanks."

"All you gotta do is tell us how you want your food and that's how you'll get it at Sally's."

"It's great," Clint said, not knowing what else to say to her.

"You enjoy. I'll bring you some more coffee."

"Thanks."

She started away toward the kitchen when a man came out of the kitchen. He was a workman, from the look of him. He wasn't wearing a gun, but there was a hammer tucked into his belt.

"Sally, want me to take the windows out now?" he asked.

"Shhhh!" she said, shushing him loudly. "Not here, Fred. Talk to me in the back."

They disappeared into the back and Clint wondered about what he'd just heard. Take the windows out? Is that what those other places had done? Purposely removed their windows? And did this have something to do with the man he'd met today, Simon Butcher? Did people really think they could avoid taxes by removing their windows and Butcher wouldn't know they'd done it?

On the other hand, Clint didn't know how Butcher's job worked. Would he be allowed to presume the presence of windows, even if they were conveniently missing when he showed up for his inspection?

Clint wondered how long Butcher would be around inspecting buildings. Long enough for all of the building owners to try to hide their windows?

He was going to have to ask Wiley what was going on. He wondered if, when he reached Wiley's ranch, his house would be without windows.

Clint finished his meal at Sally's, and when he left, her windows were still intact. He did, however, pass a couple more buildings that had them removed. He wondered if Butcher was inspecting by appointment. Certainly, if these buildings had not been inspected by the end of the day they'd have to refit the windows, or risk being robbed overnight. Lucky for them the weather was mild. Maybe Butcher ought to think about inspecting in the winter, when it was too cold for people to remove them.

Clint stopped in the nearest saloon next. It was a small establishment called the White Branch, which offered very little other than whiskey or beer. There were no gaming tables, and no girls. At this time of day, with a lot of people still working, it was empty but for three or four men who either didn't want to work, didn't have to, or simply didn't have jobs.

Clint was halfway through a cold beer when he found out that he'd been wrong about the place having no girls. He heard the sound of voices, male and female, and then two men with two women came down the stairs from the second floor. They were laughing, and it was pretty obvious what they had been doing upstairs with the girls, who worked for the saloon—which, by the way, still had windows.

One of the men was telling a story while the other man and the two women kept laughing.

"You shoulda seen him," the man said. "He

jumped off that buckboard so fast he just about fell on his face."

"Well," the other man said, "serves him right for raising taxes the way he does."

The two men leaned on the bar and ordered beers, then pulled the two women close.

"Does he raise the taxes?" one of the women asked.

Clint looked closely at her. She was in her late twenties, with long dark hair and beautiful, smooth skin. She was not laughing as hard as the others.

"What?" the second girl asked. "Of course he does. Haven't you been listening, girl?"

"Seems to me he just does the inspections," the woman said.

"And he sends in his report," the second man said, "and then your taxes get raised."

"So he doesn't do it," she said.

"Of course he does," the first man said, and then he looked around and added, "but not for long around here. We scared him good."

"Mighta scared him better if that other fella hadn't come along," the second man said.

"Hey," the first man said, "we coulda took care of him, too."

"Mr. Fairburn said no one else was to be involved," the second man said.

"Fairburn be damned!" the first man said. "We coulda took that other fella. We didn't have ta let him spoil our fun."

"Well," the second man said, "maybe you're right."

"I ever see him again," the first man said, "I'll fix him good."

Clint dearly hated braggarts, and these two were being about as loud about it as you could be. They both looked trail-hardened, with worn guns tied down, but their actions earlier in the day told him that they needed a pack behind them to back their play.

He was about to prove it.

"Say that again?" he called out.

"What?" the second man said.

"Whozat?" the first man said, turning to look over his shoulder.

"That was me out there, this afternoon," Clint said.

"That was you doin' what?" the first man asked.

"Ruining your fun, as you put it," Clint said. "Me, I don't think five against one is fun. Let's see how you feel about two-to-one odds, though."

"Mister," the first man said, "what are you talkin' about?"

"You said if you ever saw the man who ruined your fun again you'd fix him," Clint said. "I heard you, the rest of these men heard you." He looked at the bartender. "You heard them, didn't you?"

"Mister," the bartender said, "I don't want no trouble—"

"See?" Clint said. "He heard it, too. Well, here I am, gents." Clint stepped away from the bar. "Come and fix me."

# THREE

The two men stared at Clint for a few seconds and then the second man said warningly, "Hey, Bly—"

"Shut up!" Bly said. He pushed the girl away, the older one who'd been halfway defending Simon Butcher.

The second man did the same, pushed his girl away. The first man turned to face Clint.

"Whataya mean ruinin' our fun?" he asked.

"I told you," Clint said. "Five against one is lousy odds."

"Whatayou care? What business is it of yours?"

"I make it my business whenever somebody's outnumbered," Clint said.

"But he was in the wrong."

"Says you."

"Says everybody," the man called Bly said. "Mister, you ain't from around here, you don't know what's going on."

Clint made a show of thinking for a moment, then

said, "Something about windows, I think?"

"It's more than windows, mister," Bly said. "It's money. It's people losing their places."

"Oh, so you're involved because you want to help people?" Clint asked.

"That's righ—"

"And not because somebody named Fairburn is paying you?"

"Hey," Bly said, "we gotta have jobs."

"And your job calls for you to go after a man with four other men backing you up?"

"Hey, what I do is my business," Bly said.

"Hey, mister," the second man said, "we don't want no trouble. We was just doin' our job, ya know?"

"Well, that man is only doing his job, too," Clint said. "For that he shouldn't have clowns like you shooting at him."

"Who you callin' a clown?" Bly demanded.

"You, Mr. Bly," Clint said. "I'm calling you a clown."

"We gonna let him get away with this, Sam?"

"Bly," Sam said, "I don't want no trouble."

"He's not with you, Bly," Clint said, "and neither are your other friends. You want me to wait for you to go and find four others to back your play?"

Bly's eyes narrowed.

"You push hard, mister."

"Then push back, Bly," Clint said. "I'm right here. Push back."

The other men and the two women in the place watched carefully from the sidelines, waiting for Bly to make up his mind. As it happened, the other man made it up for him.

"I'm leavin', Bly," Sam said, heading for the door. "You comin'?"

"Stop there, Sam!" Clint barked.

Sam froze and stared at Clint.

"Mister, I said I didn't want—"

"I don't want you behind me with your gun. Take it out and drop it to the floor."

"But—"

"When I leave," Clint said, "you can come back and get it. Now do as I say—and don't get between me and your friend."

Sam complied. He took his gun from his holster and dropped it to the floor, then hurriedly went out the door.

"Now you, Bly."

"What?"

"Either drop your gun," Clint said, "or use it."

Bly stared at Clint for what seemed to most of the people in the place a long time. Clint, on the other hand, was willing to give the man all the time in the world to make the right decision.

Finally, grudgingly, Bly took his gun out slowly.

"Just put it on the bar, Bly, and walk out."

Bly placed his gun on the bar, watching Clint the whole time.

"This ain't over," he said.

"I know," Clint said. "I guess I'll be seeing you sometime down the line when you've got a half a dozen men behind you."

Just for a split second Clint thought he might have pushed too hard. He watched Bly's eyes, because that's where the man's move would start, but finally Bly started walking. He went past Clint toward the door, and the closer he got to the door, the quicker his step became.

Finally, he was gone, and Clint heard a few people let out their breath.

Clint picked up Sam's gun and put it on the bar next to Bly's.

"Anybody here friends of theirs?" he asked the room.

If any of them were, they weren't admitting to it now.

Clint looked at the bartender.

"When they come back, give them their guns. For now, put them under the bar."

"Yessir."

"Hey, mister."

Clint turned and saw one of the girls standing next to him. She was blond, and younger than the other by about five years.

"You want to buy me a drink?"

"Sorry," he said, and then looked past her at the dark-haired girl, "but I'll buy your friend one."

"Her?"

"That's right, her," Clint said. "What about it?" The question was directed to the dark-haired girl.

"Sure," she said. "Sure."

"Hmph," the blonde said, and stalked off.

# FOUR

Clint and the dark-haired girl walked to a back table and sat down.

"You're probably going to have to talk to the sheriff," she said.

"That's no problem," he said. "What's your name?"

"Emily. Why did you do that?"

"Do what? Ask you your name?"

"No," she said, "help the window inspector."

"He was being shot at by five men," Clint said. "That's not fair."

"And you believe in what's fair?"

"Absolutely."

"Who are you?"

"My name's Clint Adams."

Her eyes widened.

"I know you!"

"Do you?"

"I mean, I know who you are," she said. "You—you could have killed those men."

"Probably."

"Why didn't you?"

"I didn't have to."

"You only kill when you have to?"

"That's right."

"But your reputation . . ."

"Reputations are slightly exaggerated sometimes, don't you think?"

"I wouldn't know," she said with a smile. "I've never had one."

"Well, take my advice," he said, "and don't get one."

"Why not?"

"You waste a lot of time either trying to live up to it," he explained, "or trying to live it down."

"And which did you do?"

"I've done both."

"Which one are you doing now?"

"Now," he said, "I'm just ignoring it."

"Are you going to be in town long?"

"A few days. I'm visiting a friend."

"A woman?"

He shook his head. "An ugly man."

"Maybe somebody I know?"

"Wiley Wilcox."

"I've seen him around town."

"Not a customer?"

She smiled.

"No."

"His wife will be glad to hear it."

"What about you?"

"What about me?"

"Are you going to be a customer?"

"No."

She frowned.

"Why not? Don't I appeal to you?"

"Sure you do, but that's one thing I don't pay for."

"Really?"

"Really."

"Never?"

"Well," he said, "maybe in my misspent youth, but not for a very long time."

"Well . . ." she said. She finished her drink and stood. "Then I have to go to work."

"How about another drink?"

They both heard someone enter. She turned and they both saw the badge on the man's chest. He walked to the bar and engaged the bartender in conversation.

"I don't think you have the time."

"Sure I do."

"Then I guess you'll have to have it with the sheriff. Excuse me, Mr. Adams."

"Clint."

She smiled.

"Clint."

"See you later, Emily."

As she walked away from his table, the sheriff started walking toward it.

# FIVE

"Can I talk to you for a minute?" the sheriff asked.

"About what?"

"I understand there was some trouble in here a little while ago."

Clint shrugged.

"Not very much, Sheriff . . . ?"

"Lake," the lawman said, "Sheriff Ted Lake."

Lake was in his forties, and in appearance was not so different from the two men Clint had tangled with earlier, Bly and Sam.

"What did you hear, Sheriff?"

"That you threatened to kill two men."

"And I'll bet one of those men told you that, huh?" Clint asked. "Was it Sam or Bly?"

"Did you know them before you came here?"

"Never met them before."

"Then what was the trouble?"

"The trouble is over, Sheriff," Clint said. "Nobody got hurt. Why are you interested?''

''I'd like to avoid any trouble in the future,'' Lake said. ''Bly said you were pushing him to draw on you.''

''That's not exactly true,'' Clint said. ''I was pushing him to either give up his gun or use it.''

''Why?''

''Do you know who Simon Butcher is?''

''Butcher!'' Lake said. ''Everybody around here knows who he is.''

''Bly and four of his friends thought that five-to-one odds were pretty even. They ambushed Butcher just south of town.''

''Did they kill him?''

''No.''

''Too bad.''

''That doesn't sound like an attitude a lawman should have,'' Clint said.

''Don't get me wrong,'' Lake said. ''If they had killed him, I'd have arrested them, but I wouldn't have shed any tears for the window inspector.''

''The man is just doing his job and everybody wants to kill him for it.''

''Sounds to me like he should get into another line of work.''

''That should be his choice.''

''Are you a friend of Butcher's?''

''No,'' Clint said. ''I just met him when I ran Bly and his four brave friends off. When I got to town Bly and his friend Sam were bragging to a couple of the ladies about what they did.''

''And you took exception to that?''

''Yes.''

''Why? What business was it of yours?''

"They made comments about me."

"By name?"

"They don't know my name."

"Come to think of it," the sheriff said, "I don't either."

The sheriff continued to stare at Clint expectantly.

"My name is Clint Adams."

The sheriff took one inadvertent step back, as if someone had pushed him.

"What's the Gunsmith doing in Truxton?" he asked.

"Visiting a friend."

"And getting involved in something that's none of your business."

"I'll tell you what I told Bly," Clint said. "I don't like long odds. All I did was try to even them up some."

"Bly's not gonna forget what you did, Adams," the sheriff said. "You humiliated him in front of other people."

"He's alive."

"He's not gonna forget," Lake said again.

"Is he a friend of yours, by any chance?" Clint asked. He wondered now if the sheriff was one of the other men with Bly earlier in the day.

The sheriff hesitated a moment, then said, "I know him."

"Then you better give him some good advice, Sheriff."

"Like what?"

"Like learn to forget," Clint said. "It'd be healthier for him."

"I don't want any trouble here, Adams."

"Tell that to your friend, Sheriff," Clint said. "I'm just here to visit a friend."

"And who would that be?"

"Wiley Wilcox."

"I know Wilcox," Lake said. "Where are you staying?"

"At the hotel."

"Maybe you should stay with your friend."

"Are you running me out of town, Sheriff?"

"No," Lake said after a moment, "it was just an idea, a suggestion."

"I'll be staying in town, Sheriff," Clint said. "I'd advise you to do your job and keep Bly and his friends away from me. I don't like bushwhackers, and I don't like their friends."

"That—that almost sounds like a th-threat."

The sheriff was nervous and trying not to show it.

"Not a threat, Sheriff," Clint said. "Just an idea . . . a suggestion."

# SIX

After the sheriff left the saloon, Clint leisurely finished his beer, not wanting anyone to think that the sheriff might have run him off.

When he left the saloon he walked to the livery and saddled Duke.

"Goin' back out so soon?" the liveryman asked.

"I'm in the mood for a ride."

"Looked to me when you came in that you came a long way."

"I did."

The liveryman watched Clint mount up and ride out, then shrugged and went back inside. No accounting for people.

Clint knew that Wilcox's place was only a mile out of town. He could ride there, visit, and ride back before dark. By then he'd be ready to try out that bed in his hotel.

Wilcox's spread was not a large one. The man had

settled only a few years ago after years on the trail. He'd met a woman, married, and she had settled him down. By now Clint figured he'd have a few head of cattle and some horses, if he knew Wiley Wilcox. The man was a hard worker when he put his mind to it.

He came within sight of the Wilcox place and saw just what he'd expected to see. A log house, not large or small, that Wilcox had built himself, having cut and hauled the trees himself. There was a corral with half a dozen horses in it, up against a small barn. Beyond the house a few dozen head of cattle milled about. It didn't look to Clint as if he had any hands. There was no bunkhouse, and no one in evidence. More than likely Wilcox and his wife, Kate, were running the place themselves.

As he got even closer he saw that there was a small vegetable garden up against the house, beneath a window. That was when he noticed that there *was* no glass window in the wall, just the hole and some wooden shutters. He wondered . . .

"Hey, Clint!"

He turned and saw his friend, Wiley Wilcox, coming around from the other side of the house. He looked as lean as ever. He'd thought that a wife's cooking might have put weight on his friend, but apparently the hard work had helped him keep it off.

"Wiley."

Clint dismounted and the two men shook hands. Clint noticed that there was no window on the other side of the house either. He wondered about the side and back walls of the house.

"It's good to see you," Wilcox said, pumping Clint's hand enthusiastically. Wilcox had grown a mustache since the last time Clint saw him, but the man still looked younger than his years. Clint knew he had to be close to fifty. He'd married late, and married a woman twenty years younger than he was. Clint had not known her at all, and had not been able to attend the wedding. This would be his first time meeting her.

"When did you get here?"

"Just now," Clint said.

"Where's your gear?"

"I took a room in Truxton."

"Oh, no," Wilcox said, "you're gonna be stayin' here."

"I can't, Wiley."

"Nonsense," Wilcox said. "We've got room. You'll have to sleep on the floor, mind you, but—"

"No," Clint said, cutting him off, "I mean I can't."

"Why not?"

Clint took a few moments to explain what had happened in town. He did not, however, explain about the window inspector, just that he'd had a run-in with two men.

"If I come out here to stay, two things will happen. One, folks will think the sheriff ran me off, and two, the trouble might follow me."

"Don't worry about that," Wilcox said. "My gun may have been hangin' on the wall for a few years, but I still know how to use it."

"That's not the problem."

"No, no," Wilcox said, "I understand. A man in your position can't afford to show weakness. That's generally when people attack. Well, come on. We'll put Duke up in the barn and then I'll introduce you to Kate."

"I'm looking forward to it."

# SEVEN

They went to the small barn together and made Duke comfortable, removing the saddle.

"I'm not going to be here that long," Clint had said, when Wilcox suggested unsaddling the gelding.

"At least until after dinner," Wilcox had argued. "Let's make the great beast comfortable until then."

Clint smiled. Whenever they had ridden together Wilcox had always referred to Duke as "the great beast."

Once Duke was taken care of, Wilcox took Clint to the house.

"She's heard a lot about you," he said. "Kate'll be glad to meet you."

He opened the door and Clint followed him in. What he could see was mostly one room, with a kitchen area, a table to eat, and a couple of chairs on the other side. There was a doorway that probably led to a bedroom. As he looked around he could see that there were no windows in the walls.

At the stove a woman turned. She was stunning, in her thirties, with red hair, lots of it. If it hadn't been pinned up it would more than likely have extended to her waist.

She was wearing a simple cotton dress that hugged her full body, showing off heavy breasts and wide hips. Clint was surprised. This was not the kind of woman Wilcox had preferred when they rode together. Kate Wilcox was the obvious kind of woman—built for bed—that Wilcox had avoided during his bachelor years.

She wore no makeup, but her eyebrows were full, her eyes long-lashed, and her mouth naturally red. With makeup of some kind—any kind—she would have been gorgeous.

"Kate, honey, look who's here."

"And who is this? Another mouth for dinner?"

"You bet," Wilcox said, and Clint couldn't believe that the man hadn't noticed the woman's tone of voice. "Honey, meet Clint Adams."

The look on Kate Wilcox's face changed immediately, from one of annoyance to one of great interest.

"Ah, so this is the great man himself," she said. She set the ladle she was holding down on the stove, wiped her hands on the apron that was around her waist, and approached Clint with her hand out. He took it and found her handshake to be very firm. He'd expected it would be.

"It's a pleasure to meet you, Mrs. Wilcox."

"Hey, hey, none of that," Wilcox said.

"He's right," she said. "You must call me Kate."

"All right . . . Kate."

"And the great beast? Is he in the barn?"

"Duke? Yes, he is."

"I'll have to go and see him later," she said, releasing Clint's hand. "I've heard almost as much about him as I have about you."

"Well, you can't believe everything Wiley says," Clint said.

"Oh," she said, her tone changing again, "I've found that out for myself, let me tell you."

Clint looked at Wilcox to see his reaction and there was none. He either didn't notice his wife's tone, or chose to ignore it.

"You'll be staying for dinner, of course," Kate Wilcox said.

"If it's no trouble."

She looked Clint directly in the eyes—something he liked—and said, "It's no trouble at all, Clint."

He smiled and said, "Then I'll stay."

"Then you and Wiley get out of here and let me finish cooking," she said. "I'll bring some coffee out to you."

"Thanks, sweetie," Wilcox said. He leaned over to kiss her, and she turned her head so that he had only her cheek to kiss.

"I've asked you not to call me that," she said, and went back to the stove.

"Come on, Clint," Wilcox said, "let's give the lady some room."

Outside they sat in two straight-backed wooden chairs, waiting for her to bring the coffee.

"Wiley . . . is everything . . . all right?" Clint asked.

"Oh, sure," Wilcox said, "she's just a little tired, is all. It's kind of hard trying to keep this place runnin', just the two of us."

"Can't you get some help?"

"Had help," Wilcox said. "I had three hands, but I had to let them go."

"Money?"

"Ain't that always the problem?" Wilcox asked. "You know, money never was a problem when I was riding the trail."

"I know."

"All you ever needed was enough for a room, a meal, and a drink. This . . . this is different." He spread his hands to indicate his place.

"So is being married."

"You got that right," Wilcox said. "Bein' married's the hardest thing I ever done, Clint. It's the hardest *work* I've ever done."

At that moment the door opened and Kate came out carrying two cups of coffee. Wordlessly she gave them each one and went back inside. Clint noticed that his was just the way he liked it, black and strong.

"Ain't she a beauty?" Wilcox asked proudly.

"She is that," Clint said, sipping the coffee.

"She's a good cook, too. See that garden? She makes that come up with vegetables every year. She's a great gal, Clint."

"I'm sure she is."

"But she ain't happy," Wilcox said, looking into his coffee. "Not with me, anyway."

"I thought . . ." Clint said, then stopped.

"You thought what?" Wilcox asked. "That I didn't notice? Oh, I notice, all right. I don't know who made the biggest mistake, Clint. Me for marrying someone so young, or her for marrying somebody as old as me. Whichever of us did, though, she's payin' for it."

"Wiley—"

"Nah, it's all right," Wilcox said. "I guess she'll leave me before long."

"What would you do if she did?"

"You mean what *will* I do *when* she does, don't you?" Wilcox asked. "I think I'll sell this place and hit the trail again, Clint. I miss it. I miss it somethin' fierce."

"I thought you might."

"Did you?"

Clint nodded, and Wilcox smiled.

"You mighta told me that five years ago."

"Five years ago you were in love and wanted to get married and settle down. Nothing was going to stop you."

"I guess not," Wilcox said. "I guess a man—and a woman—have got to learn from their own mistakes."

"Speaking of mistakes, Wiley . . ." Clint said.

"Yeah?"

Clint pointed and asked, "Where are your windows?"

# EIGHT

Wilcox explained about the windows over dinner. Clint noticed that Kate looked away and did not pay any attention to the conversation. On occasion, however, he caught her watching him with an expression he hoped Wilcox was not seeing.

"So after the window inspector does his inspection," Clint asked, "you'll put all the windows back?"

"That's right."

"And that works?"

"He can't tax you if he don't see actual windows in the wall."

"But . . . doesn't he know what you and everybody else is doing?"

"I guess he does," Wilcox said, "but there ain't much he can do about it."

"So let me ask you this," Clint said. "Why are so many people wanting to kill him?"

"Some people are unreasonable," Wilcox said.

"They have trouble, money troubles, and they're lookin' for somebody to blame. He's the likeliest one."

"And is it the same man every year?"

"Has been the last three years," Wilcox said. "In that time six spreads have gone under, and about that many businesses in town."

"I didn't notice any vacant buildings in town."

"That's because as soon as a business goes under there's somebody there to buy the place and start their own."

"What's this trouble you mentioned in town, Clint?" Kate asked. He hadn't been aware that she'd heard him speak of it earlier. It made him wonder how much more of his conversation with Wilcox she had heard.

"Well, it has to do with the window inspector."

He started from the beginning then, telling about how he'd helped Simon Butcher, and how that had led to the confrontation in town.

"Who were the men?" Wilcox asked.

"One fella named Bly, and another called Sam."

"Sam Dade," Wilcox said. "Bad sort, both of them, but you had them pegged. They need lots of help around them."

"Did it ever occur to you," Kate asked, "that they might kill you?"

"That always occurs to me in any situation that involves a gun, Kate."

"And yet you still stood up to them?"

"Clint can read a man better than anyone I ever knew," Wilcox said. "If he figures a man to back down you can just about bet he will."

"And would you have killed them?" Kate asked.

"If they'd forced me to."

She shook her head.

"I'll never understand men and killing. You go together like . . . bread and butter, it seems."

"I hope not," Clint said.

"I've seen enough of it, Clint," she said. "Killing comes all too easy to most. I have to admit, you showed restraint that I am not used to seeing in a man."

"Killing don't come easy to Clint," Wilcox said. "It never has. Oh, he can do it well enough when he has to, and he can face more men than I ever saw one man face, even Bill Hickok, but he don't like it. I've seen men who do, though. I've known a lot of men who just flat-out liked to kill."

"I've known a few of those myself," Clint said.

"They're the ones who should be shot down like dogs," Wilcox said.

"And you've done it, haven't you, Wiley?" Kate asked.

"I've done my fair share."

"And you're proud of it?"

"Can't say I'm ashamed of it," Wilcox said. "I killed a lot of men who deserved killin'."

She shook her head, stood up, and began to clear the table.

"Let me help," Clint said.

"Don't even think of it," she said. "Wiley, take Clint outside. When I've finished here I'll bring you each a drink." She looked at Clint. "Will you be spending the night?"

"I've taken a hotel room in town," Clint said, "but thanks."

"Won't there be trouble waiting for you there?"

"Better it waits for me there than come looking for me here."

She gave him a look then that he couldn't quite make out.

"Come on, Clint," Wilcox said, echoing words he'd spoken earlier, "let's give the lady some room."

# NINE

"You know," Wilcox said, when they were outside, "you can help me with something while you're here."

They each had a glass of whiskey, which had been brought to them by Kate. Clint's was almost finished.

"What's that?"

"After that inspector comes out here you could help me put the damn windows back. Takin' 'em out myself was hell!"

Clint smiled.

"Sure, I'll help."

"Can't sell me a house without windows, can I?" Wilcox asked.

"You've decided to sell?"

Wilcox looked at the house, but Clint knew he was seeing the woman inside.

"I think the decision will be made for me, very soon."

Clint finished off his drink and set the glass down.

"When is the inspector supposed to come out here?" he asked.

"Tomorrow, probably in the afternoon. We can start putting the windows back in after that. Why don't you come by for dinner tomorrow night, as well?"

"Okay," Clint said, "I'll be here. Tell Kate good night for me?"

"I'll tell her. Listen, I'd walk to the barn with you, but I've got some work to do. There's a fence behind the house that needs mending. I'll see you tomorrow."

Clint went to the barn and saddled Duke. He turned to lead the gelding out and saw Kate Wilcox standing there.

"You know, don't you?" she asked.

She was wearing the same dress, which still clung to her body. She had discarded the apron.

"Know what, Kate?"

"How unhappy I am," she said, coming closer. "What a sham my marriage is?"

"I'm not the only one who knows, Kate."

"You mean Wiley?" she asked. "I guess he does know, but most of the time he pretends that he doesn't."

"Maybe you and he should talk."

"We haven't talked—I mean, really talked—in so long, I don't think we'd know how."

"So what's going to happen?"

She shrugged.

"Maybe it will just come to an end by itself."

"It's my experience that very little happens by itself."

"Then maybe you can help me."

"Me? How can I help you?"

"You tell him."

"Tell him what?"

"Tell him I want him to let me go."

"I think that should come from you, Kate."

"You're right," she said. "I guess I'm just too much of a coward, but Lord knows I've been giving him hints."

"Treating him . . . badly?"

"Not badly, exactly," she said, averting her eyes, "just not . . . wifely, if you know what I mean."

"I think I do."

"Which means," she said, "that not only is he being deprived, but I am, too."

Suddenly, Clint knew what she wanted.

"Kate—"

"I don't mean here." Her hands were pressed to her thighs, plastering the dress to her even more tightly. "I could come to town. I do that sometimes."

"To do what?"

"I tell Wiley I'm visiting some friends."

"And you're not?"

"No," she said, "actually, I am."

"Men?"

"No." She shook her head. "You might not believe this, Clint, but I've never cheated on Wiley . . . not yet."

"Kate—"

"You'll be the first."

"Why me?"

"Because you're his friend."

"That should be the reason it's not me, Kate."

"We don't agree on that, Clint," she said. "I'll come to your hotel."

"No."

"Later."

"No, Kate."

She started out of the barn.

"Expect me later tonight."

"No, Kate—"

And she was gone.

What should he do? Tell Wiley? What if she was just talking? What if she didn't show up at all tonight? And if she did, who said he had to let her into his room?

If she was so unhappy, why didn't she just pack up and leave?

He walked Duke outside and mounted up. Neither Wiley nor Kate were in sight. Wiley was probably behind the house, and Kate inside. He thought about going back to talk to them, but decided against it. Instead, he turned Duke toward town and rode away.

# TEN

It was almost dark when he got back to town. He turned Duke over to the liveryman, who took him without a word. He was walking back to his hotel when he saw a familiar figure coming toward him.

It was the window inspector, Simon Butcher.

"Mr. Adams."

"Mr. Butcher."

"I thought we'd decided on first names . . . Clint."

"We had, Simon."

They shook hands and Butcher looked around to see if anyone was watching.

"What's wrong?"

"Shaking my hand is not exactly a healthy thing to be seen doing," Butcher said.

"Simon, don't worry about that. Say, don't you owe me a drink?"

"You sure you want to do that?"

"I'm sure."

"Let's find a saloon, then."

''I've been to the White Branch,'' Clint said. ''I'd like to try the other one.''

''That'd be Cahill's Saloon,'' Butcher said, shaking his head as they started walking. ''Not a lot of imagination, there. It's owned by a man named Cahill.''

''Still,'' Clint said, ''it's better than calling it the Truxton House.''

''Oh,'' Butcher said, ''that's the hotel I'm staying in.''

They entered Cahill's and it was obvious that this was the town's main saloon. There were gaming tables, and plenty of girls working the floor. It was crowded, with only some elbowroom at the bar.

''Maybe we made the wrong choice,'' Simon Butcher said.

''We can make room at the bar,'' Clint said.

''I don't mean that.''

''What do you mean?''

''With all these people,'' Butcher said, ''there's bound to be trouble.''

''I was at the other place,'' Clint said, ''and there was trouble there, already. Come on, let's get a drink.''

They went to the bar and Clint used both elbows to make room.

''Beer,'' he told the bartender, ''two.''

''Comin' up.''

The man brought two mugs and Clint paid.

''Hey,'' Butcher said, ''these were supposed to be on me.''

''You get the next round.''

''Okay.''

They drank and Clint said, "Can I ask you something?"

"Sure."

"If your job makes everybody mad at you, why do you do it?"

"Because it *is* my job," Butcher said. "It's what I do, what I'm trained to do. If I didn't do this how would I make a living?"

"There are other ways."

"Not for me."

"Well, then, let me ask you this."

Butcher waited.

"Don't you know what's going on with all these windows missing from buildings?"

Butcher laughed.

"Sure, I know."

"Then . . . what's the point of taking all the abuse you do?"

"My job is my job, Clint," Butcher said. "I get paid to do it."

"But, if you know that people are hiding their windows . . ."

"It may not go on much longer," Butcher said. "There's a possibility that by next year I'll be given more authority."

"Meaning?"

"Meaning that I'll be able to use my initiative. If I think somebody's hiding a window, I'll be able to say so in my report, and it'll mean something."

"I see."

When they finished their beers Butcher bought the second round. As Clint brought his to his lips, he saw that some men further down the bar were pointing at them and talking.

"That's him," a man said. "That there's the window inspector."

"Gonna cost me my business," another man said. "What the hell is he doin' drinkin' in here?"

"Yeah," a third man said loudly, "we got to let him into our places, but that don't mean we have to drink with him."

The three men put down their drinks and started toward Clint and Butcher.

"Here comes trouble," Clint said.

"What?"

He pointed and Butcher looked.

"Why don't you leave, Clint?" Butcher said. "No point you getting involved in this."

"I'll leave," Clint said, "when I finish my drink, and not before."

# ELEVEN

''Hey, window inspector.''

''Are you talking to me?'' Butcher asked.

''That's right,'' the man said, ''I'm talking to you. You're that window inspector.''

''I'm a homestead inspector.''

''Whatever you call yerself,'' the man said, ''you count windows.''

''That's one of my jobs.''

''What do you think you're doin' in here?'' a second man asked.

''I'm having a drink with my friend.''

The three men looked Clint over. He didn't recognize any of the three of them from the other saloon.

''And who's your friend?'' one of them asked.

''Why don't you ask him?''

''Mister,'' the first man said, ''you ought to be careful about who you drink with.''

''I am,'' Clint said, ''that's why I'm not drinking with you.''

"He got you there, Harley," one of the other men said, laughing.

"Shut up!" Harley snapped.

Harley struck Clint as the kind of man who would hang around with Bly. They were cut from the same cloth.

"You got a big mouth, mister," Harley said, "along with bad taste in friends."

"I guess I could say the same for your friends," Clint said.

"Huh?"

"Actually," Clint went on, "you have the big mouth, while they have the bad taste in friends."

Now a few other men who weren't involved in the exchange, but who were within earshot, started to laugh.

"You lookin' for trouble, friend?" Harley asked. He didn't like being laughed at. Clint thought that being laughed at might make him mad enough to do something stupid. He decided to try to defuse the situation.

"Look, friend," he said, "we're just trying to have a beer, we're not looking for trouble."

"Oh," Harley said, "now you're backin' down."

Thinking he'd made Clint back down might make the man downright brave.

"I'm not backing down, friend," Clint said. "I'm trying to save you some grief."

"Is that a fact?"

"That is a fact, yeah," Clint said.

"Well, what if I told you me and my friends *wanted* some trouble?" Harley said. "What would you say to that?"

"I'd say you were making a big mistake."

Clint decided that the only way to keep the situation from getting out of hand was to shut this fool up.

"Well, boys—" Harley started to say, but he got no further.

Clint took a quick step forward, past Butcher, and tossed the remains of his beer into the man's face. As Harley's hands went to his face to clear it, Clint reached for the man's gun and removed it from his holster.

He put the gun on the bar and said to the bartender, "I need a refill."

"Comin' up," the bartender said.

Harley wiped his face clean and looked down at his empty holster.

"Gimme my gun!"

"Believe me, Harley," Clint said, "you're better off without it."

"I said gimme my—" He cut himself short and turned to face one of his buddies. "Gimme your gun."

"I'll shoot the first man who gives him a gun," Clint announced.

"I ain't givin' up my gun, Harley."

"Me, neither," another man said.

"Damn it," Harley shouted, "somebody gimme a gun."

"You can have yours back when you've cooled down, Harley," Clint said. "I'll leave it with the sheriff."

"You're a coward," Harley said. "You're yella."

"Sure, Harley."

"Come on, Harley," one of his friends said. "Let's go."

"I ain't leavin'!"

"You can't do nothing without a gun."

Harley thought a moment, then said, "Right, right." He looked at Clint. "Don't you go away, mister. I'll be right back."

"I'm going to finish my beer," Clint said, "and then I'll be on my way."

The man glared at him, then stormed out of the saloon, followed by his two friends.

"He's going to get a gun and come back," Butcher said.

"Probably."

"Don't you think we should leave?"

"I think it would be a good idea," Clint said. He upended his mug and drank down the fresh beer. "Ready?"

"I'm ready," Butcher said.

Clint looked at the bartender and said, "Give that gun to the sheriff."

"Sure."

"If I hear you gave it back to Harley—"

"Don't worry," the barkeep said, "I'll turn it over to the sheriff."

"Good."

They turned and left the saloon. Clint almost expected to find Harley waiting for him outside, but apparently the man had to go a ways to find a new gun.

# TWELVE

Clint decided it might be wise to walk Butcher to his hotel.

"I can take care of myself," Butcher assured him.

"It would make me feel better," Clint said. "Besides, I've got to talk to you about something."

"Oh, all right."

They started for Butcher's hotel, which was at the opposite end of town from Clint's.

"What do you want to talk to me about?"

"You're doing an inspection tomorrow."

"Your friend's place?" Butcher asked. "Wilcox?"

"That's right."

"You want me to do you a favor?"

"No, no," Clint said, "nothing like that. I want you to go ahead and do your job."

"Then what's on your mind?"

"I'd just like to know when you'll be going out there, that's all."

"Oh." Butcher seemed relieved that Clint wasn't going to ask a favor, or try to bribe him. "I've, uh, got three stops to make before his place."

"When will you be getting started?"

"Early," Butcher said. "If I can get an early enough start I should be able to finish up tomorrow."

"That's good, then."

"Why did you ask?"

"I'm, uh, going out there for dinner. Just wanted to know if you'd be done by then."

Butcher laughed.

"Going to help him put his windows back in?"

"Something like that."

"You'd better advise your friend that won't be necessary next year."

"I don't think he'll own the place next year," Clint said.

"Oh," Butcher said. "I'm sorry to hear that. I hope I'm not—I mean, I hope—"

"It's not that," Clint said. "I don't think his marriage is going to last that long."

"Oh, I see. I'm sorry."

"He just wasn't meant to settle down, I guess," Clint said. "Plus he married a much younger woman."

"That can be a problem," Butcher said. "I've seen all kinds of marriages in my business. I, uh, see the inside of lots of people's homes."

"I guess you do."

They reached his hotel.

"Here I am, safe and sound."

"I saw two of the men who were shooting at you today," Clint said.

"Really?"

"They said they were only trying to scare you," Clint said.

"It didn't seem that way."

"They said they worked for a man named Fairburn."

"That figures," Butcher said. "Fairburn owns quite a few businesses in town, and a large spread outside. It doesn't surprise me that he'd try to scare me off."

"I just thought I'd let you know."

"Thanks," Butcher said, "but Fairburn is not on my list for tomorrow. I finished him up this morning."

"Well, good luck tomorrow," Clint said.

"Enjoy your visit with your friend," Butcher said.

As the man entered his hotel lobby and Clint turned to walk away, he had no idea that this was the last time he'd see Simon Butcher alive.

As Clint approached his hotel he was alert for danger. If Harley returned to the saloon with a gun and didn't find him there, the man might come looking for him. He made it to the lobby with no problem, but as he entered there were two men waiting for him. He recognized one as the sheriff, and the other as possible trouble.

# THIRTEEN

''Adams,'' Sheriff Lake said, ''this is Paul Bodie.''

Bodie was several cuts above the men Clint had had to deal with so far in Truxton. He was in his thirties, well-dressed with a well cared for gun on his hip instead of the worn iron the other men had been wearing. He wore black leather gloves, and they looked tight enough for him to pick up a two-bit piece with no problem. The gloves matched his clothes. Everything was black, his jacket, his trousers, his hat, even his shirt—even the buttons of the shirt were black. Clint wondered if the man dressed this way for effect, or if he simply liked it.

''Don't tell me, let me guess,'' Clint said. ''You work for a man named Fairburn.''

Bodie looked surprised.

''I'm impressed,'' he said. ''How did you figure that?''

''Your clothes and gun look like money,'' Clint said. ''I understand Mr. Fairburn has a fair amount.''

"I see."

"Also," Clint said, "you've got the local law acting as a toady. That takes money."

"Hey!" Lake objected.

"That'll be all, Sheriff," Bodie said. "I'll take it from here."

Lake didn't like it, but he relented and left.

"Can we talk?"

"It's a little late."

"Actually," Bodie said, "it isn't."

"Well, it is if you've been in the saddle as much as I have today."

"I just need a few moments," Bodie said. "We can do it right here."

"All right," Clint said. "Have your say."

"I understand you interfered with some of Mr. Fairburn's men today."

"I did if this Fairburn sends five men out to bushwhack one."

Bodie frowned at Clint.

"Have you never heard of Walter Fairburn?"

"Never," Clint said. "Why, should I have?"

"He's a very wealthy man."

"Well, there are a lot of wealthy men I've never heard of," Clint said. "Are you finished?"

"Not quite. I have a message from Mr. Fairburn."

"Give it to me."

"He knows who you are, but he won't tolerate interference again."

"Fine."

"Do you understand?"

"Perfectly."

Bodie stared at Clint.

"I'm not sure you do."

"Believe me," Clint said, "I've been threatened enough times to recognize when it's being done."

"And in the past, when you've been threatened, have you heeded the threat?"

"Hardly ever," Clint said. "As a matter of fact, never."

"That could be a problem, Mr. Adams," Bodie said, "that is, if you intend on staying in town long."

"I'm here visiting a friend," Clint said. "When my visit is over, I'll leave."

"Until then," Bodie said, "I strongly recommend you stay out of Mr. Fairburn's way."

"I'll tell you what," Clint said. "You tell Fairburn to label his men so I can tell them from the rest of the townspeople, and I'll do my best to avoid them. How's that?"

"I get the impression you're not taking this little talk seriously."

"Well, then, you're very observant," Clint said, "because it's an impression I'm trying to convey."

"You know," Bodie said, "there's a possibility you'll have to deal with me."

"You'll excuse me if that means nothing to me," Clint said, "but you see, I've never heard of you, either."

With that Clint turned and left Paul Bodie standing there while he ascended the stairs to the second floor.

Bodie watched until Clint was out of sight, then turned and headed for the door, thinking, *This could be very interesting.*

Clint went to his room, wondering if Bodie might have a surprise waiting for him in there. He unlocked the door, drew his gun, and went in quickly, covering the room with the barrel of his gun.

There was somebody there, all right, but she had not been sent by Paul Bodie.

"Why do you look so surprised?" Kate Wilcox asked from his bed. "I told you I'd be here."

# FOURTEEN

"And why the gun?"

"I was expecting someone else," he said, holstering it.

She was in his bed with the sheet covering her, but it was obvious that she was naked beneath it.

"Kate," he said, "you have to leave."

"Who were you expecting?" she asked, ignoring his statement. "Paul Bodie?"

Clint stared at her.

"What do you know about Paul Bodie?"

"He's a friend of mine," she said. "I saw him in the lobby when I sneaked in."

"Did he see you?"

"No."

"What exactly do you mean when you say he's your friend?"

"We've known each other a long time."

"Before Wiley?"

"Before Wiley, and before this town."

Clint sat on the end of his bed and pulled off his boots.

"Tell me about him."

"Now you want me to stay?" she asked, wrapping her arms around her knees. The move revealed her lovely shoulders, pale and smooth.

"For a while," Clint said. "Tell me about Bodie. He seems confident."

"You mean, even when he was talking to the great Gunsmith?"

Clint didn't respond.

"Well, he is confident," she said. "He's very good with a gun."

"I've never heard of him."

She smiled.

"He keeps a low profile. He's not the kind of man who goes looking for a reputation."

"Well," Clint said, "at least he's smart."

"Oh, he's very smart."

"Are you lovers, Kate?"

"We were, once."

"Once?"

"I told you," she said, "I haven't cheated on Wiley—until tonight."

"Why not?" Clint asked. "I mean, if Bodie was available and you needed it, why not with him?"

"Because Paul Bodie's old news, Clint," she said. "You, on the other hand, are something new."

He turned to look at her and she chose that moment to lower the sheet to her waist. He caught his breath. Her breasts were beautiful, full and firm with pale pink nipples. Oddly, just about an inch above each nipple she had a strawberry mark, almost like a teardrop. He found himself fascinated by them.

"Why did you marry Wiley, Kate?"

She folded her arms across her chest and raised an eyebrow, as if she was giving the question a lot of thought.

"I'm serious."

"All right," she said. "I thought it was a good move for me, Clint. I had done a lot of things in my life, but I was getting too old to continue most of them."

"You're not old."

"I'm . . . in my middle thirties. That's a little old to keep relying on your looks."

"I think you could rely on your looks for a long time to come."

She smiled.

"Thank you, but there are some things I am too old for—if you know what I mean."

He thought he did.

"Do I shock you?"

"No," he said, "not much shocks me anymore, Kate."

"Well, the prospect of being a madam didn't appeal to me, and then Wiley came along. He told me he was going to build a big spread and I believed him. I didn't know it would be like this."

"It takes time to build the kind of spread Wiley was talking about, Kate."

"Well, I don't have that kind of time to spend, Clint," she said. "I've got to get out."

"Well, don't look at me."

She laughed and opened her arms to show him her breasts again.

"I don't want you to take me away with you,

Clint," she said, "I just want you to take me away tonight."

"Kate . . . Wiley's my friend."

"It's not like you're taking anything that he wants, you know."

"Any man would want you."

"Including you?"

"Including me," he said, "if you weren't married to Wiley."

"Clint," she said, "Wiley hasn't touched me in two years. I had a lot of sex before I met Wiley, and even during our first two years he was interested. During the third year it got less and less, and after that it just stopped."

"His decision?"

"Well . . . it wasn't exactly a decision. He just . . . couldn't."

"Oh . . ."

She tossed the sheet off of her completely and he saw the curly hair between her legs. She got to her knees and moved closer to him. He could feel the heat from her.

"Clint, I've gone just about as far as I can go without having a man touch me—and I don't want to be with Paul Bodie."

"You're saying if I don't have sex with you now you'll go to Bodie?"

"I'll have to."

"Well, that might be best," he said, after a moment. "You'll get what you want, and I won't feel like I've betrayed a friend."

She pressed herself against him then and kissed him. He was helpless. Her heat enveloped him, her tongue invaded his mouth. His hands went to her warm flesh. She tore at his shirt, popping buttons as she tugged it from him, and then her breasts were against his chest.

"Kate, I can't—"

"I can't leave now, Clint," she said, against his mouth, "someone will see me."

"Kate—"

"Come on! I want you! I want it!"

# FIFTEEN

Suddenly, with strength that shouldn't have surprised him given her size, she pushed him down on the bed. She touched him through his pants and found him hard.

"Oh, God . . ." she said breathlessly. She attacked his belt, undid it, and pulled his pants and underpants from him. His erection stood out and she grabbed it in both hands.

He couldn't believe how good it felt when she took him in her mouth. All thoughts of resistance fled as she began to suck him, holding him with one hand while the other teased his balls and touched him elsewhere.

"Mmmm," she moaned, sucking him avidly.

He looked down just as she looked up at him. She released him from her mouth and regarded him with a smile. Slowly, she stuck out her tongue and licked him, then took the head of his penis into her mouth and sucked it. She took more of him then and continued to look up at him. Finally, when she took him all the way into her mouth she couldn't maintain eye contact, but that was okay because he had closed his eyes by then and was himself moaning.

She released him again but kept him pressed to her mouth. He looked down at her.

"I want this in me," she said, licking him again.

She moved up on him, reached for him with her hand, and guided him into her. She sat down on him, engulfing him fully and almost crying out.

"Jesus, I'd forgotten . . . my God, you fill me up!"

She started to bounce up and down on him then, faster and faster, her breath coming in hard gasps. He reached beneath her to cup her buttocks. Her breasts were bouncing in front of his eyes and he couldn't take his eyes off of them.

"Oooh, God, oh, God, oh, God, this is soooo good," she said, over and over, "so *good*, so *good*," putting the emphasis on the word "good" each time she came down on him.

Suddenly, Clint decided that he would control this situation she had virtually forced him into.

With his hands still on her buttocks he lifted her off of him.

"Wait, no," she said, "I don't want—"

He pushed her off of him roughly. She hit the mattress close to the edge and fell off the bed with a thud.

"What—"

"Let's take this to the floor," he said.

He got on the floor with her and kept her from getting up.

"What are you doin—"

"Just lie still," he said. "You said you wanted this, now you're going to get it."

He grabbed her ankles, pulled her toward him, spread her, and impaled her on his penis. She gasped as he entered her and began pounding away at her, still holding her ankles, still holding her spread-eagled.

"Jesus," she said, growing more excited. She had never been manhandled this way before.

Clint felt the excitement, too. He had never dominated a woman in quite this way before. He was angry at her for forcing this, but at the same time he had never felt this kind of excitement before. It was like they were both animals.

She was staring up at him from between her own legs. Her body was covered with sweat and was glistening. Her nostrils were flaring, she was biting her lip, and still Clint wanted her to feel more.

Abruptly, he pulled out of her.

"Oh, no," she begged, "don't—"

He got down between her legs and touched her with his tongue. She jumped, as if jolted by lightning. He thrust a finger into her while he licked her and she cried out.

"Oh, God, oh . . . oh . . . oh shit! What are you—oooh!"

He inserted a second finger and began to suck on her, and before long her stomach trembled and she was thrashing about on the floor, drumming her heels and fists on the wood as he held her there and continued to suck on her even while her body was wracked with spasms of pleasure she'd never felt before.

"Oh, God . . ." she said again, her body taut, and then suddenly she went limp.

But Clint wasn't finished.

He got to his knees, grabbed her ankles again, and rammed himself into her. She was so sensitive at this point that pleasure and pain were comingling. She wasn't sure she could tell where one began and the other ended, but she knew one thing for sure.

She didn't want this to end.

# SIXTEEN

Clint drove himself into her again and again, and this time he was interested in only one thing. His own pleasure, his own release.

She began to breathe hard again, a short, raspy sound that would leave her with a sore throat for a while. Her own pleasure began to build again.

Clint released her ankles so that her legs dropped to the floor. He put one hand on either side of her to support his weight and continued to drive into her. Her arms and legs came up around him, and their sweat caused their bodies to make slapping and sucking sounds as their flesh slapped together and then "sucked" apart.

"Come on, damn you!" she rasped at him. "Come on."

He couldn't believe her. After all he'd given her she still wanted more. He began to think that with this woman he'd never be in control. If this was what she was like after going two years without sex—or was this what she was like *because* she had gone two years without it?

He didn't have time to dwell on it. His own release was getting closer and closer, and he decided not to fight it. Suddenly he was ashamed of what he was doing. No amount of justifying on Kate's part could persuade him that he was not betraying his friend by having sex with his wife, no matter how unhappy their marriage was.

He continued to drive into her until he exploded and, with a loud groan, emptied himself into her. . . .

"Oh, God," she said, for the hundredth time, it seemed.

They had gotten off the floor and onto the bed and were lying side by side, trying to catch their breath.

"It's never been like that for me," she said.

He didn't respond.

She looked at him, then put her hand on his thigh.

"Are you angry with me?"

"No," he said, "I'm angry with myself."

"Clint," she said, "I was determined that this was going to happen, from the first moment I saw you."

"I could have resisted."

"No," she said, "you couldn't have—and I'm not being immodest. I'm just saying that I wanted this so badly I would have done anything to make it happen."

"Anything?"

"I would have blackmailed you into it, if I had to."

"How?"

"I would have threatened to tell Wiley we had sex,

even if we hadn't," she said. "So you see, you really had no choice."

"Somehow, that doesn't make me feel better."

They were silent for a few moments before Kate spoke again.

"Wiley doesn't expect me home tonight."

Clint didn't respond.

"May I sleep here?"

"Sure," he said, "but that's all we're going to do the rest of the night, sleep."

"That's fine with me," she said. "You wore me out. Remember, I haven't done this for a while."

"Just go to sleep, Kate," he said. "In the morning you can go back home to Wiley, or go wherever you want to go."

"Oh, I'll go home," she said. "I'm not ready to leave just yet. Wiley and I will have to work out the details. I'm not going to leave this marriage with less than I had coming in."

"That's up to the two of you."

"Besides," she said, "you're coming over for dinner tonight, to help him put the windows back, aren't you?"

"Yes."

"Don't worry, Clint," she said, tightening her hand on his thigh, "Wiley will never know. I swear."

"Go to sleep, Kate."

Kate removed her hand from his thigh, turned onto her side with her back to him, pulled the sheet up to her neck and said, "Good night."

Clint felt so bad he didn't think he'd be able to

sleep with her in the bed, but if he'd worn her out, the same was true of him. He was so tired from the day, and from what had just happened, that he fell asleep in minutes.

# SEVENTEEN

Clint woke the next morning with a groan and then realized that Kate was between his legs and had him in her mouth. She was sucking him, sliding her mouth up and down the length of his penis while she held the base with one hand. With the fingers of her other hand she was stroking his anus and he groaned again but didn't push her away.

She worked on him until he exploded into her mouth, and she continued to suck until he was done.

"Why did you do that?" he demanded when she released him from her lovely mouth.

She smiled sheepishly and said, "I figured you couldn't be madder at me than you were when we went to sleep. Besides, I woke up and you were lying there naked, and your penis was stiff and beautiful, and I couldn't resist you. I just had to gobble you up."

"Jesus . . ." he said. She was so frank that he felt himself reacting to her again. This was an incredibly sensuous woman, not at all the type of woman Wiley Wilcox was used to. Clint wondered if she had simply intimidated him into a state of impotence, or if there was something physically wrong with him.

"Kate?"

She moved up alongside him and lay down, almost touching him.

"Hmm?"

"Did Wiley see a doctor?"

"You mean about . . . his problem?"

"Yes."

"No. He's too ashamed to admit it to anyone, even a doctor."

"Then it could be something physical."

"It could, I suppose," she said, "but that's not going to make a difference, Clint. It's over between Wiley and me, no matter what happens from here on out. I know that now. This night with you has made me see that I have to break it off while I'm still young enough to make a life with someone else."

Well, he couldn't fault her for wanting to be happy. He could only fault himself for being too weak to deal with her. He consoled himself with the knowledge that hardly any man would have been able to resist what she had offered during the night, and in the morning. And despite his reputation, and what people and newspapers had said about him over the years, he had always maintained that he was just a man, like any other.

Didn't this prove it?

"I have to go," she said, sitting up.

He compounded his sin by watching her dress and enjoying it.

"I've never had a man watch me dress before—not with so much pleasure."

"It's a small thing," he said. "I've always enjoyed watching women dress—or do anything."

"You're a man who loves women, aren't you, Clint Adams?"

"I can't deny that."

"Too much to ever settle with one, I'll bet."

"Guilty, so far."

"Did you ever consider it?" she asked.

"Once," he said, "or twice, no more."

"Who were the women?"

"Friends."

"Are they still around?"

"One is," he said, thinking of Anne Archer. "One's dead." That was Joanna.

"I'm sorry."

She finished dressing and faced him.

"I'll see you this evening, then?"

"Yes," he said. "I'm not going to pull out on Wiley now . . . not after . . ."

She moved to the bed, touched his cheek, stroked it.

"Try not to be so hard on yourself," she said. "When I was younger I was a hard woman to resist."

"You still are, Kate," he said, "and you know it."

"I know it," she said, "now. That was something I had to prove to myself, Clint."

"Well," he said, "you proved it to both of us, didn't you?"

"Yes," she said, "I suppose I did."

With that she turned and left the room. Clint turned over and tried to go back to sleep, but her scent was everywhere. He got dressed and went downstairs for breakfast, but before he sat down he stopped at the desk and asked the clerk to have the sheets on his bed changed, immediately!

# EIGHTEEN

Over breakfast Clint found himself wondering if he'd be able to face Wiley Wilcox that evening after having spent the whole night with his friend's wife. Kate had said that she couldn't resist his stiff dick that morning, but it was stiff because he'd been dreaming about her. In his dreams he had replayed the scene on the floor. The two of them straining at each other, groaning and moaning aloud, sweating and grunting—even now he felt himself stiffening.

He called the waiter over and ordered more coffee. His steak and eggs had been tasteless, but the coffee was good. He decided that he'd take the rest of his meals at Sally's; the food had been better there.

When the waiter brought the second pot of coffee, Clint asked the man if he could find him a newspaper.

"Local?" the man asked.

"Whatever."

The waiter left and returned with two newspapers. The local paper was the *Truxton Journal*, and it was a day old. The other was the *Arizona Herald* and was several weeks old.

"Where did this come from?" Clint asked. "This is Missouri."

The waiter shrugged.

"It was in the back so I brought it out. Some drifter probably left it."

Clint wondered why they'd been saving the paper. Did they expect the person to come back for it?

He set the *Herald* aside and read the local paper while he drank the second pot of coffee.

There were a couple of small stories in the newspaper about small homesteads that were going up for sale. Nothing was said about foreclosure, so Clint assumed that the owners were anticipating a tax raise that they couldn't handle and had decided to sell out.

There was also a story about a business in town that had changed hands. The buyer was a man named Walter Fairburn.

Clint wasn't sure why Fairburn had sent Paul Bodie to brace him, and thanks to Kate he hadn't had much time to consider the question. Now he did. When and where had he gotten in Fairburn's way, he wondered, other than saving Butcher from Bly and the other four men? Could that incident, coupled with his face-off with Bly in the saloon, have been enough for the man to want to warn him off? Did Fairburn think that he could avoid paying taxes on his many holdings simply by scaring off the homestead inspector?

Surely a man who had amassed the wealth he apparently had could not be that stupid.

Could he?

• • •

Clint left the newspapers behind for the next person who wanted something to read. He had not even opened the Arizona paper. What was the point?

He was at somewhat of a loss for something to do between now and dinner at Wiley Wilcox's. He settled for a walk around Truxton. That didn't take long, and it wasn't particularly revealing. At least nobody tried to shoot him for having a drink with Simon Butcher.

Thinking of Butcher, he wondered how the inspection of Wilcox's place would go. Not that it mattered. As soon as Kate and Wilcox talked, the place would be on the market and Wilcox would take to the trail again. He wondered how long Butcher's other stops would take him and where they would be.

Thinking of Wilcox made him feel guilty all over again. He decided to find a chair someplace, sit in it for a few hours, and then head out to help Wilcox put his windows back in. If he could do that without the guilt overcoming him, then he could get out of town the next day and put the Butcher/Wilcox/Kate experiences behind him.

Lately, stopping in to visit old friends was becoming a chore.

# NINETEEN

From his second floor office window Walter Fairburn looked down at the main street of Truxton. Behind him Paul Bodie stood, waiting.

"Keep Bly away from Adams."

"Okay."

"Where's Butcher?"

"He left his hotel early this morning."

"Is someone watching him?"

"Yes."

Fairburn turned to look at Bodie, unaware that Clint Adams was walking beneath his window at that moment. He had not seen Clint since his arrival in town, but had only heard about him.

"Is Adams going to be a problem?"

"Not unless we make him one."

Fairburn frowned.

"I'm aware that you didn't approve of my sending you to talk to him."

"I didn't approve of you sending me to *threaten*

him," Bodie said. "A man like that does not back down from threats. Neither does he react kindly to them."

"You didn't threaten him, did you?"

"I did not speak to him in a threatening tone," Bodie said, although he wasn't quite sure that was true. "The meaning was clear, however."

Fairburn's frown deepened.

"I'm not used to dealing with men like him."

"I am."

"Are you?" Fairburn asked. "Did you have men like the Gunsmith back East?"

Bodie smiled tightly.

"There are men like him everywhere."

"He has quite a reputation."

"I know."

Obviously, Bodie was not impressed with Clint Adams's reputation. Fairburn liked that about the man. However, he was also not impressed with his employer, and Fairburn didn't like that. What kind of man was not impressed by money?

"What do you want done about Adams?" Bodie asked.

Fairburn sat in his leather chair and regarded the other man.

"I suppose I should defer to you on this, shouldn't I, Paul?"

"It would probably be wise."

"Very well, then," Fairburn said. "You handle the problem."

"It isn't a problem, yet."

"Well," Fairburn said, "when it becomes one, you handle it."

"Very well."

"Now, what about Wilcox?"

"He's not ready to sell."

Fairburn firmed his jaw, which meant he wasn't very happy. Bodie had worked for him long enough to read his expressions.

"I want that land, Bodie."

"I know it. Maybe you can force him to sell."

"Maybe," Fairburn said, "and maybe the men who work for me can show a little initiative. Do you think?"

"It's entirely possible."

"That's all, then."

Bodie turned without further word and left the office.

Fairburn turned his chair and stared out at the sky. The building he was in was the tallest in town, so there was nothing to obstruct his view.

He simply sat, and stared.

When Paul Bodie got down to the street he pulled on a pair of black leather gloves. He was dressed entirely in black today—as he was every day. He liked black. It was how he felt, it was how he wanted people to see him.

He found Clint Adams interesting. In truth, he had run into no one like the Gunsmith during his years in the East. Since coming to the West, the same was true. He was sure that Clint Adams was one of a kind, just as he was. That was what made the situation so intriguing.

He didn't look for trouble, though, so he wouldn't be approaching Clint Adams unless he got in the way—again. If and when that happened maybe he'd send Bly in again, let him get killed by Adams. It would give him even more of a reason to handle things personally.

# TWENTY

When Clint reached Wiley Wilcox's place he found Kate waiting for him, but no Wilcox.

"Where did he go?" Clint asked Kate when she told him that Wilcox was not there.

"I don't know," she said. "He just saddled his horse and rode out."

"Did you have a fight?"

"No."

"You didn't talk to him about . . . you know . . ."

"No!" she said firmly. "I'm not ready for that yet, and neither is he."

"Then what happened?"

"I don't know, Clint."

He looked around, wondering if he should look for Wilcox or just unsaddle Duke and wait.

"Dinner will be ready in half an hour," she said. "Why don't you give him until then before you start to worry?"

"You're not worried?"

"No."

"Has he done this before?"

"Yes," she said. "He rides off all the time to be by himself."

That made Clint feel better, although not by much. Wilcox knew he was coming for dinner. Why would he ride off like this?

"Clint, why don't you take care of your horse and come inside? I'll give you a cup of coffee."

"I'll be right in."

He unsaddled Duke and left him in the small barn, then walked to the house. He noticed that the windows were still missing.

As he entered the house he asked, "Has the inspector been here today?"

"Yes," she said. "He came about an hour ago, did what he had to do, and left."

"And when did Wiley leave?"

"Just after the inspector did."

Clint frowned as she handed him a cup of coffee.

"Why don't you sit down?"

He sat at the table and watched as she poured herself a cup of coffee. She looked much the same as she had the day before, with a simple dress and apron. However, he still saw the woman who had been on the floor of his room, her ankles in his hands, her legs spread apart as far as they could be, and he thrusting himself into her. . . .

He pushed away thoughts of last night. If she were any other woman, he'd have her on the floor of the kitchen already. . . .

Again he pushed away his thoughts of her and replaced them with thoughts of Wilcox. When he looked at her she was smirking, as if she knew the difficulty he was having.

"What did the inspector say, Kate?"

"I don't know," she said. "I didn't listen. He and Wiley walked around the house together for a while, then went outside."

"Did you ever hear them raise their voices to each other?"

"No," Kate said, "why would they?"

"I don't know," he said. "I'm just wondering why Wiley would leave so soon after the inspector did."

"Well," she said, "I'll tell you one thing."

"What's that?"

"If he's not back I'm not helping to put these windows back in."

Clint didn't respond.

"And I'm not waiting dinner for him," she went on. "We'll just eat without him. I don't want this roast drying out."

"You made a roast?" he asked.

"With plenty of vegetables."

His mouth started to water and for the first time he noticed the delicious smells in the air. The dinner last night had been good, but not elaborate. It seemed that tonight she was trying to impress him.

With her cooking, that is. . . .

# TWENTY-ONE

When the dinner was ready they sat down and ate. Clint felt badly eating without Wilcox, but after sleeping with his wife the night before he figured how much worse could this be?

"Do you still regret last night?" she asked, from her seat across the table from him.

Clint stopped eating and looked around, as if expecting Wilcox to appear at that moment.

"Yes, I do, Kate."

"I don't," she said, leaning her arms on the table. "It was . . . wonderful, amazing, in fact."

"Kate—"

"I want to do it again."

"No!"

"Oh, I don't mean right away," she said. "After Wiley and I are divorced, couldn't we . . . meet somewhere?"

Clint actually found himself giving it some

thought. Where was the harm after the divorce? Then he roughly pushed the thought away.

"I don't think that would be a good idea, Kate."

"Oh, I do," she said, eyeing him lasciviously. "I think it would be a marvelous idea."

"Could we not talk about this now?"

"Fine," she said, "we'll talk about it after the divorce."

"Kate—"

"Would you like some more coffee with your dinner?" she asked innocently, like a perfect hostess.

"Sure," he said, holding out his cup.

When dinner was over Clint went outside to wait in front of the house for Wilcox. By the time Kate had finished cleaning up and joined him, the man still hadn't returned.

"Now I'm getting worried," she said.

"Are you, really?"

"Well, of course," she said. "We may not have a happy marriage, Clint, but that doesn't mean I want anything to happen to Wiley."

"I should go look for him," Clint said. "Maybe he fell off his horse or something."

"You do that and I'll wait here."

"If he comes back," Clint said, "don't let him leave again."

"And if you find him," she said, "drag his sorry ass back here and maybe I'll give him something to eat."

Clint nodded. He could see in her eyes that she was actually worried, and was covering it up with her words.

"I'll bring him back," he promised.

• • •

Clint wasn't quite sure where to look for Wilcox. If the man had been between the house and town he would have passed him along the way—unless Wilcox knew a shortcut to town. He should have asked Kate about that.

He could check for tracks, but the main road had plenty. He got his bearings, tried to figure where a shortcut might be, and left the road. He searched for a half an hour and came up empty. At least he didn't find his friend lying on the ground hurt somewhere.

He started to backtrack, wondering where he should look next. There were three other directions to pick from the house, but it would take him hours to make a thorough search. Maybe he should just go back to the house.

He started that way, then realized that he was turned around. He was heading away from town and away from the house. His concern for his friend had gotten him a bit lost. He sat astride Duke, taking a few moments to get his bearings. When he thought he knew the way back to the house he started riding. He'd gone a hundred yards when he saw something. It was a buckboard, and it had been overturned. The horse that had been pulling it was gone. He wondered if it could be the same buckboard . . .

He rode quickly to it and saw that his worst fears were true. There was someone lying on the ground next to the overturned buckboard. If it was Wiley . . .

But it wasn't. He could see that as he drew closer. Even as he dismounted and went to examine the body he knew what he would find.

A dead man named Simon Butcher.

# TWENTY-TWO

Clint turned Butcher over and saw that he had been shot twice in the chest. What had he been doing this far from the road? Was it the same men from the day before who had shot him?

He stood up and looked around. From the tracks on the ground he surmised that there had been two horses in the area. One had been Butcher's horse, and the other a rider's animal. There was nothing remarkable about the rider's tracks that would help him identify the horse.

He thought about putting Butcher's body on Duke's back, but it was a long walk either way, to town or to the house. His best bet was to go for help. He decided to go back to the house and get one of Wilcox's horses to use to transport the body back to town. He could either put the body on the horse's back, or hitch the animal up to the buckboard. If Wilcox had returned, between the two of them they could right the buckboard and load the body onto it.

It never occurred to him at that moment to wonder if Wiley Wilcox had had something to do with this. He was fairly certain that the killer had to be one of the men he had run off the day before, perhaps even Bly. He'd have to talk to the sheriff about it.

For now, he mounted Duke and started back to the house.

When he reached the house he could tell by the fact that Kate was sitting outside that Wilcox had not returned. He rode right up to the house.

"Did you find him?" she asked, standing.

"No," he said, dismounting, "but I found something else."

"What?"

"A dead man."

She displayed shock.

"Who?"

"Simon Butcher."

She frowned.

"Who is that?"

"The homestead inspector."

Her eyes widened.

"The window inspector?"

Clint nodded.

"What happened to him?"

"Somebody shot him, twice."

"Do you think it was Wiley?"

Now it was his turn to show surprise. The thought had never occurred to him.

"No," he said. "Why would you ask that?"

"I don't know," she said, shrugging. "The question just occurred to me."

Clint wondered who else the question might occur to.

"Why did you come back?"

"I need a horse to take the body into town."

"Well, help yourself."

"You better stay here, Kate, in case he comes back."

"And if he doesn't?"

"Maybe he's in town."

"Maybe something's happened to him, too."

That made more sense to Clint than thinking Wilcox had anything to do with Butcher's death. What motive could he possibly have had for that? He wasn't looking to hold on to this place anyway, so Butcher's report wasn't going to hurt him that much.

"What do I do if he doesn't come back?" she asked. "I want to know what's going on."

"If you decide to ride into town," Clint said, after a moment, "then leave a note for him."

"Good idea," she said. "I'll wait as long as I can and then come to town to see what's going on."

"Okay."

"Clint?"

"Yeah?"

"Be careful, will you? If someone shot this man Butcher, they might try to shoot you, too."

"I'll be careful."

# TWENTY-THREE

When Clint rode into Truxton with the body of Simon Butcher tied to the back of a horse, he attracted a lot of attention. Eventually he reached the sheriff's office, and Lake came out to see what the commotion was.

"Who's that?" he asked.

"Simon Butcher," Clint said, dismounting.

"Who?"

"The homestead inspector."

"Oh," Lake said, "the window inspector?"

"That's him."

Lake walked over to the body and lifted the head by the hair to look at the face.

"That's him, all right. How'd he die?"

"He was shot," Clint said, "twice in the chest."

The sheriff turned and looked at Clint.

"Did you do it?"

"No."

"Who did?"

"I don't know," Clint said. "I found him."

"Where?"

Clint waved and said, "Out there, somewhere. I got turned around."

He didn't want to say that he'd found the body anywhere near Wiley Wilcox's place.

"Okay," Lake shouted, "since you're all milling around, I need a couple of men to take this body to the undertaker's."

No one volunteered, so he pointed to two men and told them to do it.

"Whose horse is this?" Lake asked as the two men walked the horse to the undertaker's.

Now Clint was stuck. He could tell the truth, or lie. If he lied and got caught it would look like he was trying to cover for his friend.

"It belongs to Wiley Wilcox."

"Was he with you when you found the body?"

"No."

"Then why do you have one of his horses?"

"Butcher's buckboard was overturned and his horse was gone. I needed some way to get him back to town, so I borrowed a horse from Wiley."

"Well," the sheriff said, "I'll see that he gets it back."

"That's fine."

"Would you come inside with me, Adams?"

"What for?"

"I'll tell you inside," Lake said. "Please?"

"Sure, why not?"

Clint preceded Lake into the office while the sheriff shouted for the crowd to disperse.

In his office Lake walked around behind his desk.

"I hope you don't mind, Adams," he said, "but I'll have to take a look at your gun."

Clint hesitated. He knew the man was intimidated by him, but in asking for his gun he was just doing his job. He had to admire him for that.

"Okay," he said, and handed it over.

Lake took the weapon and sniffed it. It smelled neither recently fired or recently cleaned. He handed it back.

"Just checking."

"You'll want to check my rifle, too."

"Yes."

Clint went out and got it, brought it inside. The sheriff tested it the same way, with the same results.

"Satisfied?" Clint asked.

"Yes," Lake said. "I'm just doing my job."

"I know that. Is there anything else?"

"Do you have any idea who might have shot him?"

"You might ask your friends, Bly and—what's his name?—Sam, and their friends."

"Why?"

"They had Butcher pinned down yesterday, before I ran them off, if you'll remember."

"That doesn't mean they killed him."

"I guess that's for you to find out, isn't it?"

"I know my job, Adams."

"I don't doubt that you do," Clint said, and thought, *But that doesn't mean you're going to do it.*

"If you're done with me, I'll be going," Clint said.

"Where?"

"Back to my hotel, for now. After that, I don't know."

"Just don't leave town without letting me know . . . okay?"

"Sure, Sheriff."

Clint left the sheriff's office and walked to his hotel.

"Any messages for me?" he asked the clerk.

"No, Mr. Adams," the man said. "Were you expecting something?"

"No, that's okay."

He hadn't expected anything, but he'd hoped to find a message from Wilcox. Now he had to wait for Kate to arrive in town, hopefully with Wiley Wilcox in tow.

Clint went back outside, found a chair, and seated himself in front of the hotel.

Attracted by the commotion, Paul Bodie had come out of the saloon, where he was having a beer, and saw Clint Adams in front of the sheriff's office. He watched as the horse carrying the body was led to the undertaker's, and then as Clint Adams went into the sheriff's office. In a few moments he came out again, took his rifle from his horse, and went inside. No doubt the sheriff was doing his job.

Once Clint was back inside the sheriff's office, Bodie left the saloon and walked down to Walter Fairburn's office to let his boss know what was going on.

# TWENTY-FOUR

Clint was still sitting in front of the hotel when Kate Wilcox rode into town. She was wearing riding clothes, and riding a well-muscled steeldust, not the kind of horse you would expect a lady to be riding.

She reined the horse in, tied it off, and stepped up onto the boardwalk with Clint.

"He never came home."

"And he's not here."

"What do we do now?" she asked.

"I don't know," he said. "Has he ever stayed away overnight before?"

"Only when he got drunk and played poker," she said, "and he hasn't done that in over a year."

"Well," Clint said, standing up, "let's go and see if there's a poker game going on."

"I don't think he'd go and play poker when he was expecting you to help him put those windows in."

"Maybe not," Clint said, "but let's check anyway."

"Fine."

"Let's take your horse over to the livery first."

"I probably should get a hotel room for the night," Kate said, as they walked the horse to the livery stable, "shouldn't I?"

"Yes, you should."

"Unless you want to share—"

"We'll get you your own room."

"I didn't bring any money."

"You can owe it to me."

"What about clothes?"

"You can wear the same clothes tomorrow," he said, "and go right home and change."

"The same clothes?" she asked, aghast. "Obviously you've never been married."

"Never."

"The same clothes . . ." she said. "The idea . . ."

They left her horse at the livery and then went to the two saloons in search of a poker game. There was not one in evidence, so they asked the bartender in the White Branch if he knew of one.

The man was staring at Kate, so Clint had to snap his fingers to get his attention.

"Oh, a game?"

"Maybe a private game?"

The man thought, then shook his head.

"Not that I know of."

"Have you seen Wiley Wilcox in town today?" Kate asked him.

"That's who you are," the bartender said. "Wiley Wilcox's young—I mean, wife."

"That's right."

"I haven't seen him."

"Does that mean you haven't seen him," Kate asked, "or does that mean you haven't seen him because I'm his wife?"

"It means I ain't seen him," the bartender said.

Clint looked at Kate and said, "Do me a favor and wait outside."

He could see she wanted to protest, but she didn't. Instead, she turned and walked out.

"Look, Wiley might be in some trouble," Clint said.

"Trouble with his wife?"

Clint shook his head and said, "Trouble with his life."

"Serious, huh?"

"Yeah, serious."

"Well," the bartender said, "if I *had* seen him I wouldn't have told his wife, but I really haven't seen him."

"Are you telling me the truth?"

"Mister," the bartender said, leaning on the bar, "I saw you face Andy Bly down right here in this bar, him and Sam Dade both. Yeah, I'm tellin' you the truth."

"Okay," Clint said, believing the man, "thanks for your help."

He went outside where Kate was waiting, her arms folded beneath her breasts.

"Well?" she asked.

"He hasn't seen him."

"He's lying," she said. "He's covering for that bastard, worrying us like tha—"

"He might have lied to you," Clint said, "but not to me. He hasn't seen him."

She calmed down a bit, but her arms stayed folded. "What do we do now?"

"Well, we could go to the sheriff."

"We can't do that."

"Why not?"

"Well, number one, because he's a moron," she said, "and number two, what if Wiley had something to do with that man's death?"

"That's the second time you said that, Kate," Clint said. "Did they have an argument?"

"No."

"Then why do you think he might have killed him?"

"I don't know," she said. "I told you before, the thought pops into my mind."

"Well, not mine."

"That's because you're his friend."

"You're his wife."

"Well," she said, "you know him better than me, I guess."

Clint stared at Kate for a few moments and thought, sadly, that that was probably true. Married to the man for five years, and she apparently didn't know him all that well.

"Let's go back to the hotel," he said.

She smiled and dropped her hands to her side. "What did you have in mind?"

"I had in mind getting you a room," he said, "and then getting some dinner."

"That's all?" she asked.

"That's all, Kate."

"Well, fine."

• • •

They walked back to the hotel, got her a room, then went to the dining room for dinner.

"The food's not too good here, but if Wiley comes looking for me, he'll come here."

"If he doesn't go home looking for me, first."

The waiter came over and took their order. Clint told him to bring a pot of coffee right away.

"You're making me out to be such a bad person," Kate said.

"Hey, I was in my room with you last night, wasn't I? What we did was not good."

"It wasn't?"

"You know what I mean."

"Well, that's not what I mean," she said. "I mean you're making me sound bad because I think maybe Wiley killed that man."

"You're not giving me any reasons."

"Well, let's look at the facts, then. The window man left our place and never got to town. Wiley left our place right after the window man, and never got to town. The next thing you know, you find the window man dead. What does that tell you?"

"That means maybe Wiley's dead, too," he said. "Maybe the same person who killed Butcher—"

"Who?"

"The window man—maybe the same person who killed him killed Wiley."

"So where is Wiley's body? Why wasn't it there with what's-his-name's, the window man's?"

Clint didn't have an answer for that.

He wished he had.

# TWENTY-FIVE

Clint and Kate were coming out of the dining room when Clint saw Bly—whose first name he now knew was Andy—coming down the steps from the second floor. Bly saw him at the same time and surprised Clint by going for his gun.

Clint's quick reaction, despite his surprise, saved his life—and possibly Kate's. With his left hand he pushed her out of the line of fire, while he drew his gun with his right. Bly cleared leather but never got a chance to bring the gun up. Clint shot him in the chest twice. The man tumbled down the steps and was dead before he hit the lobby floor. Papers that he was holding in his hand went flying and fluttered to the floor around him.

"What the hell was that all about?" Clint demanded loudly.

"I'm gettin' the sheriff," the desk clerk yelled, and ran out. He had ducked behind the desk when he saw what was going to happen, and consequently he didn't see exactly what had happened. All he knew was that there was a dead man on the floor.

"What happened?" Kate asked, regaining her feet. Clint's shove had knocked her to the floor, out of harm's way.

Clint walked to Bly and checked him.

"Is he dead?" Kate asked.

"Yep."

"But . . . why did he do that?"

"I don't know," Clint said. "We had some words before, the day I got here, but I didn't think he was so upset he'd go for his gun the minute he saw me."

"What are these?" Kate asked, picking some papers up off the floor.

Clint picked some up, as well, and examined them.

"These look like reports," he said, "and they're signed by Simon Butcher."

"Who?"

"The homestead inspector."

"Oh, the window man?"

"Yes."

"Well, what was this man doing with them?"

Clint looked at her.

"It looks like he was stealing them, doesn't it?"

"But why?"

"That's a good question."

Clint dropped the papers on the floor, and Kate followed his example.

"Do you think this means he killed the window man?" she asked.

"I don't know," Clint said. "I guess that's for the sheriff to find out."

"For me to find out what?" Sheriff Lake asked, entering the lobby at that moment.

"Who killed him," Clint said, pointing at the dead man. He noticed that the clerk had not returned with the sheriff.

"Who is it?"

"Take a look."

Lake walked to the body, bent over it, then straightened up.

"Bly."

"Yes."

"And you killed him?"

"Yes."

"Why?"

"He tried to kill me."

"Why?"

"Well, I suspect it had something to do with these papers."

"What are these papers?" Lake asked.

Clint picked one up and handed it to the lawman. "You'll notice the signature."

Lake squinted.

"Is that . . . Butcher?"

"Simon Butcher."

"Who's that?"

"The homestead inspector."

"Oh, the window man," Lake said. "These papers belonged to him?"

"So it seems."

"And Bly had them?"

"Yes."

Lake studied Bly for a moment, then looked up the steps.

"He was coming down the steps with these papers in his hands . . ."

"That's right."

"And what happened?"

"He saw me, I saw him, he drew his gun, I shot him."

With his foot Lake turned the body over.

"Twice in the chest."

"Yes."

"Isn't that how the window man was killed?"

"Simon Butcher," Clint said, "yes."

"I guess it's a good thing your gun was unfired when I tested it earlier, Mr. Adams."

"I don't have any motive to have killed Butcher, Sheriff," Clint said. "I had a motive to kill Bly."

"The confrontation in the saloon the other night?"

"No," Clint said, "the fact that he was trying to kill me."

"The desk clerk says he didn't see anything," Lake said. "He says he ducked down behind the desk."

"So he did."

"What did you see, Mrs. Wilcox?"

"It's just like Clint said," Kate announced. "That man drew his gun as soon as he saw us. Clint pushed me out of the way and shot him."

Lake looked around and saw Bly's gun on the floor across the room.

"He got his gun out?"

"Yes," Clint said, "but he didn't get off a shot."

"Bly wasn't that quick."

"I wasn't expecting him to pull his gun," Clint said. "I didn't think he'd do that the minute he saw me."

"Mmmm. Well, I guess I better get somebody to remove the body."

"Am I free to go?"

"Sure," Lake said. "Bly was a hothead. This is the kind of thing he would have tried. Besides, Mrs. Wilcox is your witness, isn't she?"

"Yes," Kate said, "I am."

They started for the door, and Lake turned and called, "Mrs. Wilcox?"

Clint and Kate turned and she asked, "Yes?"

"What were you doing here?"

"Having something to eat with Mr. Adams."

"And where is your husband tonight?"

"I don't know."

"Tell me something. When did the window man come to your place?"

She looked at Clint and he nodded.

"Today."

"And when did he leave?"

"Around four."

"Is your husband home?"

"I can't really say, Sheriff," Kate said. "After all, I'm here, aren't I?"

"Are you staying in town tonight, Mrs. Wilcox?"

"As it happens," she said, "I am."

"Trouble at home?"

"That's none of your business, is it, Sheriff?"

Lake studied her for a moment, and then he said, "I guess it isn't. Okay, thanks."

On the way out the door Clint said to her, "That was very good."

# TWENTY-SIX

"What do we do now?" Kate asked.

"This doesn't make sense," Clint said.

"What doesn't?"

"Bly trying to kill me on sight."

"He was stealing," she said, "and we saw him. Maybe he was afraid you'd tell the sheriff."

"But *what* was he stealing?" Clint asked. "Not money. Not anything valuable."

"Why was he stealing those papers, then?"

"Who does Bly work for?"

"Walter Fairburn."

"Directly?"

"Well, no . . . he works for Paul Bodie."

"So then either Bodie or Fairburn must have sent him to steal the papers."

"So that Butcher's reports wouldn't be sent in after his death?"

"Maybe."

"But why?" she asked. "Won't they just send

somebody else to do the reports again?''

''Maybe they will,'' Clint said, ''and maybe it'll be somebody who would take a bribe.''

''You think Butcher wouldn't?''

''I think Butcher liked his job too much to.''

''So you're saying that either Fairburn or Paul had Bly kill Butcher?''

''Or they were simply taking advantage of his death to steal his reports.''

''Maybe you should go and talk to them?''

''Why?'' Clint asked. ''That's the sheriff's job.''

She made a rude noise with her mouth.

''What's that mean?'' Clint asked.

''It means Lake won't do anything to upset Fairburn. He's not going to ask him any questions.''

''Well, it's still not my job.''

They were walking along, heading nowhere in particular.

''What if they killed Wiley, too?'' she asked. ''Would you ask questions then?''

''Yes,'' Clint said, without hesitation. ''Wiley is my friend.''

''Well, we can't find him,'' she said. ''What if he's dead, and we don't know it?''

''First you thought he killed Butcher, and now you think he might be dead?''

''I don't know what to think.''

Clint took a deep breath and let it out in a sigh.

''No, neither do I,'' he said. ''Why don't we go and talk to Mr. Fairburn?''

''It's late,'' she said. ''He won't be in his office.''

''Do you know where he lives?''

She nodded.

# TWENTY-SEVEN

"Mrs. Fairburn?" Clint said to the woman who answered the door.

"Oh, heavens, no," she said. "I'm the housekeeper." She was in her fifties, a plain woman wearing a housecoat.

"I see. Is Mr. Fairburn home?"

"Yes. He's in his study, but it's late—"

"Would you ask him if he'll talk to me, please?" Clint said, interrupting her. "My name is Clint Adams."

The woman looked pointedly at Kate, but neither she nor Clint offered her name.

"I'll go and ask him," she said. "Wait here, please."

The women went off and returned moments later.

"Follow me, please."

Clint and Kate followed her into the house and down a hall. The house was on the edge of town, a two-story wood frame, well built and expensive.

"Mr. Adams?"

The man behind the desk was tall, barrel-chested, in his fifties. When he saw Kate Wilcox his expression changed, becoming more cordial. "I'm sorry. I thought you were alone."

"Do you know each other?" Clint asked.

"We've met. Hello, Mrs. Wilcox."

"Mr. Fairburn."

Fairburn looked past Clint to the housekeeper.

"That'll be all, Mrs. Casey."

"Yes, sir."

She backed out of the room and closed the door.

"My wife died some years ago," he explained. "I find I need a housekeeper. Please, sit down. What can I do for you?"

"Do you employ a man named Andy Bly, Mr. Fairburn?"

"Bly?" Fairburn repeated the name. "I can't say positively, but the name sounds familiar."

"You don't know who works for you?"

Fairburn laughed, totally relaxed.

"I have a . . . well, if I had a ranch I guess you'd call him a foreman."

"Paul Bodie."

"You've met?"

"You should know," Clint said. "You sent him to threaten me."

"Did I?" Fairburn cocked his head to one side. "I don't recall doing that."

"Maybe it was his idea."

"I'll have to talk to him about it."

"To get back to Bly," Clint said, "he's dead."

"Oh, my," Fairburn said, sitting up straight. "And how did that happen?"

"He tried to kill me."

"I see. And you killed him?"

"Yes."

"Well, fortunate for you, I suppose."

"Is that all you have to say?"

"Well, considering I'm not even sure the man worked for me, what else could I say?"

"I suppose you heard about Simon Butcher being killed?" Clint asked.

"Butcher? Who's that?"

"The homestead inspector," Kate said.

"Oh, the window fellow. Yes, I heard about that."

"And I suppose you don't know that Bly was one of five of your men who had Butcher pinned down yesterday."

"I don't have any knowledge of such an incident, Mr. Adams," Fairburn said. "Do you mind if I ask you a question?"

"Sure, go ahead."

"Why are you asking me these questions and not the sheriff?"

"I don't know, Mr. Fairburn," Clint said. "I suppose you'd have to ask him that."

"Yes, I suppose I will," Fairburn said, "but what I don't think I'll do is answer any more of yours. Good evening, Mr. Adams. It was nice to see you, Mrs. Wilcox."

Suddenly, Kate stood up and leaned on the man's desk.

"Do you know where my husband is?"

"I'm sure I don't, Mrs. Wilcox."

"Did you have him killed, too?"

"Too?" he asked. "I don't recall having *anyone* killed, let alone your husband. Is that what this is about? You people think that I have people killed?''

''Do you?'' Clint asked.

''I'm a businessman, Mr. Adams,'' Fairburn said. Then he looked at Kate and added, ''And I have no idea where your husband is, or what's happened to him, *if* anything has happened to him.''

''Where's Paul Bodie now, Mr. Fairburn?'' Clint asked.

''I'm sure I don't know, Adams,'' Fairburn said, ''but that sounds like a good idea. Go and talk to Paul.''

''I will.''

''You should be warned, though,'' Fairburn said, ''he is neither as polite nor as patient as I am.''

At the door Clint said, ''I'll keep that in mind.''

When they were outside the house Kate asked, ''Well, what did that accomplish?''

''He didn't like being questioned,'' Clint said. ''If he's the kind of man we think he is, he'll probably send someone after me.''

''Like Bly?''

''Somebody better than Bly.''

Kate hesitated, then asked, ''Paul?''

''Why don't we find him and ask him?''

# TWENTY-EIGHT

"He'll be in a saloon at this time of the night," Kate said.

"You know him that well?"

"I did, once," Kate said. "It's my opinion that men don't change much, Clint."

"You thought Wiley would change when you married him, didn't you?"

"No," she said, "I knew Wiley wouldn't change."

"Then why did you marry him?"

She shrugged and said, "I thought I'd change, but I didn't."

They reached the center of town and Clint asked, "Okay, which saloon?"

"Paul likes noise and people when he's not working," she said.

"Cahill's."

• • •

They walked into Cahill's and Clint checked the bar. He'd been careless with Bly and didn't want that same thing to happen again. The last time he was in here he'd also had an altercation with some men and taken a gun away from one of them. If they were here now they might want a rematch.

"There he is," she said.

Satisfied that the men were not there, he looked at her and asked, "Where?"

"Over there," she said, pointing.

It took him a moment but he finally located Bodie in the crowded saloon. The place was so crowded that few of the men had even noticed that a woman had entered.

Paul Bodie was sitting at a table alone, except for a saloon girl and a beer.

"Maybe you better wait outside," Clint said.

"Why?"

"A couple of reasons," he said. "Men are going to notice you, and that'll attract attention to us."

"And the second reason?"

"I think he'll act differently when you're around, don't you?"

"Probably," she said. "He's been trying for months to get me to go to bed with him, whenever I'm in town."

"So you'll wait outside?"

"Yes," she said, "but not for long. I'll get lonely out there."

"I won't be long."

"Better not be, or I'm coming in," she said.

"Fair enough."

She went back out through the batwing doors and he made his way to Bodie's table.

"Hey, Adams," Bodie said. "Want a beer? Hazel, here, will go and get it, won't you, honey?"

"Sure, Paul."

Clint looked at Hazel. She was young, maybe twenty-two or -three, very pretty with red hair and pale skin. She had a sprinkling of freckles across the expanse of breasts she was showing, and she was showing enough to determine that the freckles went a long way.

"I'll have a beer," Clint said. "Thanks, Hazel."

"Go and get it, baby," Bodie said, and patted her on the rump as she went by him.

"Have a seat, Adams," he said. "Kate decide to wait outside?"

"I asked her to," Clint said, sitting across from him. He figured Bodie was the kind of man who would have noticed them as soon as they walked in.

"Why?"

"I didn't want her to get in the way of what we were going to say."

"And what are we going to—?"

He stopped when Hazel returned with Clint's beer and put it in front of him.

"Run along now, Hazel," Bodie said. "Pay attention to some of the other customers."

"Okay," she said, putting one hand on his shoulder, "but I'll be back."

"I'll be here."

He reached up and patted her hand before she went away.

"So?" he asked, picking up the conversation from where they'd left it.

"Andy Bly is dead."

Bodie stared at him long enough for Clint to realize that he hadn't known. He didn't look surprised, though.

"I'm not surprised," he said, as if reading Clint's mind. "How'd it happen and how do you happen to know about it?"

"I happen to know about it because I killed him."

"Now, how did that happen?"

"We were in the lobby of my hotel," Clint said.

"You and Kate?" Bodie asked with a smirk.

"We'd had some pie and coffee together in the dining room," Clint said. "When we came out Bly was coming down the steps. He saw me and went for his gun."

"Bad mistake," Bodie said. "Fatal, obviously. What was he doing in your hotel?"

"I thought you'd know that."

"Why would I know that?"

"Because he worked for you."

"He still had time of his own," Bodie said, "and as you can see, I'm not working now. So, what was he doing there?"

"He had some papers in his hand when I killed him."

"Papers?"

Clint nodded.

"They were reports written by Simon Butcher."

"Who?"

"The home—the window guy."

"Oh, him. So I guess that means Bly killed him, huh?"

"Does it seem that obvious to you?"

"Not to you?"

"No."

"Well, maybe it will be obvious to the sheriff."

"Which means he won't be looking for a killer anymore."

Bodie laughed.

"It wouldn't matter if he was looking. Lake could no more find a killer than he could find . . . well, anything."

"You don't seem to have much confidence in the sheriff."

"I don't."

"Why is that?"

"Because he's a moron."

That seemed to be a popular opinion around town.

"Well, if you came here looking for me to tell you something I don't know, Adams, I guess you're out of luck. I've been here for hours. Hazel can tell you that when she comes back."

"That's a good alibi."

"I don't need an alibi."

"It's a lucky man who has one even when he doesn't need one," Clint said, standing up.

"You haven't touched your beer," Bodie said.

"I'm really not thirsty."

"Or maybe you don't think I'm good enough to drink with?"

"You wouldn't be trying to pick a fight with me, would you, Bodie?"

"Now why would I go and do a thing like that, Adams? I have no reason to."

"I talked to your boss tonight."

Bodie frowned.

"At his house," Clint said.

"What'd you say to him?"

"You fellas will have to compare notes later,"

Clint said. "Right now I've got a lady waiting outside."

"And where would the lady's husband be about now?" Bodie asked.

"Funny, I thought you might know that, too, but you don't seem to know much, do you, Bodie?"

Bodie smiled and said, "I know when not to know anything, Adams. It's a gift."

Clint decided to let the man have the last word, and went out to keep Kate from getting lonely.

# TWENTY-NINE

"Well? Did you learn anything?"

"Only that he knows when not to know something."

Kate looked puzzled.

"What?"

"It's a gift."

"What are you talking about?"

"I'm talking about a man who claims to know nothing."

"That's not like the Paul Bodie I knew."

"Well, maybe he's changed."

"You forgot my rule, Clint."

He stared at her.

"Men don't change."

"Ah, you're right, I did forget."

"Where do we go now?"

"There's not much else that can be done tonight, Kate. I'm for turning in."

"This early? Don't you want to do some man stuff first?"

"Man stuff?"

"Get drunk, play poker, chase women?" she asked. "Isn't that what men like to do when the sun goes down?"

"I've got a Robert Louis Stevenson book in my room to read."

"Really? I *love* Stevenson! We could read it together."

"No."

"We could read to each other."

"No."

"You're going to leave me in my room all alone?"

"You'll be safe."

"But lonely."

"Maybe your husband will show up."

She made a face and said, "I'd still be lonely. Wiley's not much of a talker, and he sure doesn't read."

She was right. The Wiley Wilcox he remembered wasn't much of a reader.

"I'll tell you what I'll do."

"What?" she asked anxiously.

"I'll loan you the book."

She pouted and said, "How big of you."

"Kate, I told you—"

"I know," she said, interrupting him, "you told me that what happened last night between us was not going to happen again."

"That's right."

"While I'm married to Wiley."

"I didn't say that."

"No," she said firmly, "you're right. You didn't. I did."

Bodie gave Clint and Kate time to get safely away from the saloon before he got up to leave.

"Hey!" Hazel said, catching his arm. "You said you'd be here."

He took her hand, kissed it, and said, "I'll be back, sweetie. I promise."

This was the night he had promised himself he would bed Hazel, and he wasn't going to let Bly getting killed ruin it.

When the housekeeper showed Bodie to Fairburn's study, Fairburn said, "I've been expecting you. Did he find you?"

"Adams? He did."

"Then you know about Bly."

"Yes."

"Why did you send that fool?"

"I didn't think he could possibly mess it up."

"Well, he did."

"There's no real problem here."

"Oh? What about those papers?"

"The sheriff will have them."

Fairburn raised an eyebrow.

"You're right."

"I'll have them in the morning."

"And what about Wilcox?"

"What about him?"

"I think it's time for him to be arrested for the window man's murder."

''I can take care of that in the morning, too.''

''Well, see that you do, then,'' Fairburn said, ''and do it yourself, Bodie. I don't want this messed up.''

''Don't worry,'' Paul Bodie said, ''it won't be.''

# THIRTY

Clint had taken Kate to his room, made her wait in the hall, then came out and gave her the book.

"Are you sure . . ."

"I'm sure," he said. "Good night, Kate."

"Are we getting up early in the morning?" she asked.

"I'll knock on your door. We'll have breakfast early and try to figure out our next move."

"All right, then. Good night."

He watched as she walked down the hall and let herself into her room, then he went into his own room. As he had asked that morning, fresh sheets had been put on his bed. So why was he still able to smell Kate in the room? Maybe her scent was on his clothes, from having spent the entire evening with her.

He took off his boots, socks, and shirt and lay on the bed in his Levi's. Even if he'd had the Stevenson book he didn't think he would have been able to concentrate. There was too much going through his mind.

Where was Wiley Wilcox?

Who had killed Simon Butcher? Andy Bly? Was his killing Bly the end of that investigation? Or did Sheriff Lake have no intention of mounting an investigation of any kind? Was he incapable of it, anyway?

And what was he doing here in his room alone when Kate was down the hall?

Damn Wiley Wilcox anyway for marrying a woman so much younger than he was, not to mention beautiful and passionate. He wondered what would have happened if he had met Kate before she married Wilcox. Not that he would have wanted to marry her himself, but Wilcox certainly would have seen that she was not the woman for him.

Then the question would have been, would Wilcox have listened to him?

Looking at Kate, what would the chances of that have been?

He was about to douse the lamp and try to get some sleep when there was a light knocking at the door. There was no doubt about who it was. When he opened the door Kate was there, fully dressed.

"Kate—"

"Do you have an extra shirt?" she asked. "I can't sleep in these clothes and expect to wear them again tomorrow."

"Sleep naked," he said, before he could stop himself.

"Is that an invitation?"

"No," he said, "but come on in and I'll see if I have a clean shirt you can sleep in."

She came in and closed the door behind her.

"It doesn't have to be clean," she said. "I can sleep in the shirt you wore today. Where is it? Here it is."

She picked it up off the bed and held it to her face, inhaling deeply.

"At least I can have your smell in bed with me."

"Are you sure?" he asked, looking in his saddlebags. "I have two clean ones here."

"No," she said, shaking her head and holding his shirt behind her back, "I want this one."

"Okay, then," he said, "take it."

He went to the bed and sat on it.

"Haven't been to sleep yet?"

"Uh, no. I've been thinking."

"About me?"

He hesitated, then said, "Among other things."

"Ooh," she said, "honesty. I'm not used to that in my—in men."

"Come on, Kate," he said. "You're as worried about Wiley as I am."

She sat on the bed with him, but on the other side so that he had to turn to look at her. She held his shirt in her lap.

"I want a divorce from him, Clint, but I want him to be all right as much as you do. I *like* Wiley, I'm just not in love with him. I never was. I made a big mistake, and it cost us each some years."

"If it's any comfort," Clint said, "I think he's as ready to call it off as you are."

"Did he say that?"

"He knows you're not happy," Clint said, "and he misses the trail."

"I thought so. Sometimes I'd catch him staring out

the window, or sitting in front of the house, staring off into space.''

''So this will be the best thing for both of you.''

''That's good,'' she said, smiling. ''We'll both be happy for a change.''

''What will you do after the divorce?'' Clint asked. ''Where will you go?''

Her first instinct was to make a joke about him wanting to know where to find her, but instead she answered seriously.

''I think I want to go to a big city,'' she said. ''Denver, or San Francisco.''

''How about New York?''

She wrinkled her nose and said, ''New York? I think the thought of that scares me. That might be too big.''

''You could handle it.''

''You think so?''

''I know so.''

''You've been there, huh?''

''Many times,'' he said, ''but I've been to Denver and San Francisco, also.''

''Which do you prefer?''

He thought a moment, then said, ''San Francisco. I like it better as a city, and there's more for me there.''

''The hotels? Gambling houses?''

''Yes.''

''Houses of ill repute?''

''I don't go to whorehouses, Kate.''

''Really?''

''I don't like paying a woman to have sex with me,'' he said. ''If a woman's in bed with me I like knowing that she's there because she wants to be."

"Well, I can vouch for that," she said, raising one hand. "I think any woman would want to be. I know I want to be."

"Kate—"

"You know," she said, exasperated, "for the most part you being unlike any other man is good, but any other man would be in bed with me in a minute if I asked."

"I know," he said, "and don't think I don't want to be."

"Wiley?"

"Wiley."

She looked down at the shirt she was holding and said, "I might as well go back to my room, then."

"I'd appreciate it."

"I think if I took off all my clothes you'd take me to bed."

"I think so, too."

"But I won't."

"Why not?"

She stood up and said, "You said it, already. The next time I go to bed—or the floor—with you, I want it to be because you wanted it—without me forcing you."

"You didn't force me."

She wrinkled her nose again and said, "Yeah, I did."

"Yeah, you did," Clint said, "sort of."

"Night, Clint."

"Good night, Kate."

She got up and left, taking his shirt with her.

He stripped down to his underwear, doused the

lamp, and crawled into bed with the crisp new sheets. She'd been in the room, though, and her scent seemed everywhere.

Damn it!

# THIRTY-ONE

At eight a.m. Clint knocked on Kate's door. She answered it, wearing his shirt.

"Time to get up."

"Oh, God," she said, putting her hands to her face, "I must look awful."

"Well, make yourself look better," he said. "Take fifteen minutes and then meet me in the dining room."

"Fifteen minutes—" she started to protest, but he closed the door on her.

She came down to the dining room a half hour later. She was wearing the same clothes she had worn yesterday, and had probably combed her hair with her fingers, but the men in the room followed her with their eyes until she joined him at his table.

"I'm hungry," she said.

"I ordered for both of us."

"What?"

"Steak and eggs."

"Good."

"Have some coffee." He reached over and poured her a cup. "How did you sleep?" he asked.

"Lousy. What about you?"

"Badly."

"Have you given any thought to what we'll do today?" she asked.

"Some," he said. "We could go back to your place and see if Wiley came back."

"I left him a note," she said. "If he came back he would have read it and come here."

"Then we can stay in town and see if he shows up."

"If we do that won't Fairburn send Bodie after you?" she asked.

"He might."

"And if he does?"

Clint shrugged.

"We'll have to see what happens."

"You and Paul," she said. "That should be something to see."

"Where's he from?" Clint asked.

"He's from back East," she said, "but don't let that fool you. He knows how to use a gun."

"I thought he might."

"And he's killed a lot of men—or so he says."

"Have you ever seen him kill a man?"

Suddenly, she dropped her eyes. The waiter chose that moment to come with their food. They waited until he was finished and had walked away.

"Kate?"

"I saw him beat a man to death one night."

"When? Where?"

"It was years ago, back East."

"How did you happen to see it?"

She looked at him and said, "I was the reason it happened. I guess I should tell you the whole truth about Paul Bodie."

He waited.

"Back East he . . . was a pimp, for a while."

"And you were one of his girls?"

She nodded.

"I was *his* girl, he used to say. Other men could rent me out, but no man could have me but him."

"You must have been very young."

"I was," she said. "I was a virgin when I met him. He saw to that very quickly. You see, I had to run away from home because my father used to beat my mother. He used to rape her, too. When I turned fifteen he started looking at me . . . well, my mother said I had to leave before he . . . he . . ."

"I understand."

"I was on the streets for two years before Paul found me. He took me in, dressed me, taught me how to walk and talk, and then put me to work."

"How long were you with him?"

"About eight years."

"That's a long time."

"It was eight years on and off," she said. "We'd fight, I'd leave, or he'd throw me out, or he'd leave, but we always ended up back together."

"And all that time you were working?"

"I was only a prostitute until I was twenty, then he decided that he didn't want other men touching me. He put me to work in another area."

"What was that?"

"Con games," she said, looking away. "You can see I have a very checkered past."

He reached out and took her hand.

"I'm certainly in no position to cast stones, Kate," he said.

She squeezed his hand.

"Did Wiley know all this?"

"No!" she said. "I didn't see any reason to tell him originally, and then Paul . . . well, I finally left him for good several years ago, but he found me. He always finds me."

"Well," Clint said, "maybe after all is said and done here you won't have to worry about him finding you anymore."

"Are you going to kill him?"

"I don't plan to," he said, "but it would seem that he and I are on a collision course."

"You think he's behind everything?"

"Fairburn's behind everything," Clint said. "Bodie is the man who carries it all out, though."

"So what will we do today?"

At that point a man came running into the dining room. Clint recognized him as the bartender from the White Branch. He looked around, spotted Clint and Kate, and hurried over.

"I thought you would want to know, Mr. Adams," he said.

"Know what?"

"You, too, ma'am," the bartender said.

"What are you talking about?"

"I'm talking about Wiley Wilcox."

"What about Wiley?" Kate asked.

"He's in jail."

"What?" Clint said.

"Yup."

"How do you know?"

"I saw them take him into the jailhouse."

"Who?"

"Sheriff Lake and Paul Bodie."

"Bodie!" Clint said. "What did he have to do with it?"

"Well," the man said, "it looked to me like Bodie was the one who brought Wilcox in."

Clint and Kate looked at each other, then stood up and hurried from the room, leaving the bartender behind.

# THIRTY-TWO

Earlier that morning Paul Bodie rolled over in bed and looked down at the naked girl next to him. There was a time he would have been thinking about putting her to work, she was so young and fresh. Now, however, he was only thinking about taking her again.

He ran his hand down her naked back to her firm buttocks, then slid his hand between her thighs. Expertly he probed, making her wet even before she was awake. As she came awake she moaned and moved her hips in tandem with his rubbing, probing fingers.

"Oooh, God," she said into the pillow, "that feels so good."

He leaned over and kissed her shoulder blade, then the space between the two shoulder blades. He began to kiss her back, lower and lower, until he was running his tongue along the cleft between her buttocks, all the while continuing to manipulate her with his fingers.

Abruptly, he removed his fingers and she let out a different moan, one of disappointment. He didn't make her wait long. He slid down between her legs on his back and took hold of her hips. She wasn't sure what he wanted, or what he was going to do, but finally she rose up onto her knees.

"Spread your legs," he instructed.

She did so and he was then able to slide beneath, then bring her down to him so he could do with his tongue what he had been doing with his fingers.

"Oooh, what are you—oh! No one's ever done that before!"

That wasn't quite true, he thought. He'd done it last night, only from a different, more conventional angle. He was surprised at how inexperienced she was for a saloon girl, but it also delighted him.

He held her by the hips, probing with his tongue, using his lips as well, until he felt her shudder and stiffen and heard her cry out. She was very wet, and he continued to lick her even after the tremors ceased. She was sensitive, though, and jerked her hips each time his tongue touched her.

He slid out from beneath her then and said, "Stay on your knees."

He got on his knees behind her, took hold of her hips again, and then slid into her from behind. She was wet and hot and started to move back against him as he moved in and out of her. After this he would have to get dressed and leave. He had business to take care of. But not until he was finished with little Hazel. . . .

She watched as he got dressed.

"My God, Paul, how did you learn all of that?"

she asked. "You really know how to treat a girl."

"I made it a point to learn, Hazel," he said, cupping her chin in his hand, "and as long as you're a good girl I'll continue to treat you this way."

"I don't know if I can take it," she said, her eyes wide and shining. "My legs are weak."

"You go back to sleep."

"Do you have to go out so early?"

"Yes," he said, "I have business."

He leaned over and kissed her. She smelled warm and sweet, and as she closed her eyes to go back to sleep he thought of how he would have liked to have had her in the old days, back East. She would have fetched a good price, night after night—maybe not as good as Kate used to, but good enough.

Kate. Thinking of Kate made him think of her husband, Wiley. Why a woman like Kate would marry a man like Wilcox was beyond Paul. And why she continued to think that she could get away from him was something else again.

Hazel moved beneath the sheet, rolling onto her back. The sheet molded itself to her firm breasts and thighs, and for a moment Bodie thought about getting back into bed with her. Fairburn was paying him to do a job, though, and he was going to do it.

He left his room and went out to catch the desperado who had shot down what's-his-name, the window man.

# THIRTY-THREE

When Clint and Kate entered the sheriff's office, Lake looked up from his desk.

"I'm not surprised."

"I want to see him," Kate said.

"He's under arrest, Mrs. Wilcox—"

"For what?" Clint demanded.

"The murder of the window man."

"Butcher."

"Yeah."

"What makes you think Wilcox shot him?"

Lake didn't answer.

"Did Bodie tell you that when he brought him in?" Clint asked.

"As a matter of fact, he did."

"Is Paul Bodie a deputy now?"

"No," Lake said, lifting his chin, "just a concerned citizen."

"Where does he say he caught Wilcox?"

"Hiding out."

"Where?"

"He . . . didn't say."

"We want to see him."

Lake did his best to look officious.

"His wife can see him," he said. "She's family."

"That's hogwash, Lake," Clint said. "I want to talk to him."

Lake withered beneath Clint's stare. He'd obviously been told to keep Clint away from Wilcox, but he wasn't able to withstand Clint's will.

"Well . . . okay, but only for a few minutes."

"Fine."

"You'll have to leave your gun with me."

Clint eyed the sheriff for a few seconds, then removed his gun from his holster and handed it over.

"The gun belt, too."

Clint complied.

"Do you want to search me?" Kate asked.

For a moment Clint thought the man might say yes, but in the end he said, "That won't be necessary, Mrs. Wilcox. Follow me, please."

They followed him into the back, where the cells were. There were two of them, and Wiley Wilcox was in the far cell. He was lying on his back on a cot with his arm across his face.

"Remember," Lake said, "only for a few minutes."

"Leave us alone."

Lake hesitated.

"You have my gun, Sheriff. Leave us alone."

Lake hesitated a second more, but then turned and left the room.

"Wiley!" Kate said, taking hold of the bars of the cell. "Are you all right?"

Slowly, Wilcox moved his arm and they saw that his face was bruised and cut.

"Jesus," Clint said, "did Bodie do that?"

Painfully, Wilcox pushed himself to a seated position, but didn't get up.

"I don't know who did it," Wilcox said.

"What do you mean?" Kate asked. "What happened to you yesterday?"

"I went for a ride," he said, "to clear my head, you know? To do some thinking about . . . about us."

They waited, and then Clint had to prompt him.

"Then what happened?"

"I saw that guy, the window guy, his buckboard overturned."

"Simon Butcher," Clint said. Why was it no one could remember the man's name?

"Whatever," Wilcox said. "I went over to see what happened. He was on the ground, dead from the looks of him."

"You didn't check?"

"I got down from my horse to do that and then—bam. The lights went out."

"Somebody hit you?" Kate asked.

"I guess . . ."

"Who?" Clint asked.

"I don't know. When I woke up I was in the dark, locked up someplace. This morning Bodie came for me, said he was taking me in."

"Where were you?"

"I don't know," Wilcox said. "He blindfolded me, didn't take it off until we were near town."

"Did you tell your story to the sheriff?"

He shook his head.

"Why not?" Kate asked.

"He didn't ask. I guess I'm going to have to tell my story in court."

"This isn't going to court," Clint said. "Not if what you said is true."

"It's true."

"How did your face get bruised?"

"It was bruised when I woke up in the dark. At least, it felt bruised."

"And cut?"

Wilcox put his hand to his face to feel for the cut. "Bodie did that today."

The cut was on his cheek, below his left eye, and looked purple.

"We'll get a doctor in here for you, Wiley," Clint said.

"Sure."

Wilcox looked dejected. Clint wondered why he wasn't incensed at being treated this way.

"Wiley, what's wrong with you?" Kate asked. "Why aren't you hopping mad?" It was as if she was reading Clint's mind.

"I'm just bone-tired, Kate," he said.

"We'll get you out of here, Wiley," Clint said. "I promise you."

"Sure," Wilcox said, lying back down, "I'll just wait here."

# THIRTY-FOUR

Back in the sheriff's office Clint collected his gun belt and gun.

"He needs a doctor," Clint said.

"I don't have time—"

"We'll go for him and send him over," Kate said, cutting Lake off.

"All you have to do is let him in the cell," Clint said. "You can do that, can't you, Lake?"

"Sure," Lake said, "sure, I can do that."

"And I'll be back to make sure he's been treated for his cuts and bruises."

"He'll be treated."

"Tell me something?" Clint asked. "Aren't you curious about how Bodie came to catch Wiley?"

"All I got to do is arrest him, Adams," Lake said. "It's up to a judge to ask all those questions."

"What's his motive for killing Butcher?"

"Who—oh, the window guy. I won't know. Maybe he didn't want his taxes increased."

"A lot of people didn't want that," Clint said. "That's plenty of motive for anyone."

"Not my job," Lake muttered. "That's up to the judge."

"What about Bly?"

"What about him?" Lake asked. "You killed him."

"Don't you like him for killing Butcher?"

Sheriff Lake looked as if something had just occurred to him.

"He's got no motive," he said. "He doesn't own any property." It was as if someone had coached him, told him what to say.

"But the man he works for does," Clint said, "and in case you've forgotten who that is, Sheriff, it's Walter Fairburn."

"A man like Walter Fairburn doesn't worry about taxes," Lake said.

"Maybe not," Clint said, "maybe not."

"If that's all," Lake said, "I've got work to do. I got to send for a judge."

"You do that," Clint said, "and while you're at it, you can send for a federal marshal, too."

"We don't need no federal marshal," Lake muttered. Something else he'd been told to say, but he didn't say it with much conviction.

"We'll see about that, Lake," Clint said. He took Kate's arm and steered her toward the door. Before leaving he said, "Don't forget about that doctor. We'll be sending him over."

"I'll let him in."

"Make sure you do."

With that Clint and Kate walked out.

# THIRTY-FIVE

"What is going on?" Kate asked.

"Isn't it obvious?"

"Not to me."

"Fairburn wants Wiley to take the fall for Butcher's death."

"Does that mean that Fairburn actually killed him?" she asked.

"Or had him killed."

"By Paul Bodie?"

"Or Bly, or somebody, probably under orders from Bodie."

"And why would Paul bring him in?"

"They probably held him someplace long enough to make it look like he didn't want to be found, maybe so it'd look like he was on the run. Then Bodie comes riding in with him, acting like the hero who caught the killer."

"Some hero," she said. "We have to get him out of there, Clint."

"We will," Clint said. "Kate, why don't you go and get the doctor, tell him what's happened. Do you know him?"

"Wiley and I both know him."

"Then he'll go to the jail to treat him?"

"I'm sure he will," she said. "He's known us since we moved here."

"Good."

"What are you going to do?"

"I'm going to go and send a telegram."

"To who?"

"Sheriff Lake might not think that we need a federal marshal here," Clint said, "but I do."

"Good," she said. "Where will we meet?"

"Back at the hotel in twenty minutes."

"Fine."

"Where's the telegraph office?"

She told him, then headed away from Clint, as the doctor's office was in the opposite direction of the telegraph office.

Walter Fairburn was at his office bright and early. He watched from his window as Paul Bodie approached the building. He turned, sat in his chair, and waited. Bodie appeared moments later.

"Did you do your duty as a good citizen?" he asked.

"I did," Bodie said. "I brought the killer of the window man in."

"Excellent," Fairburn said. "And did you brief the sheriff?"

"I did," Bodie said, "but he won't stand up."

"Probably not," Fairburn said, "but he'll send for a judge. That's all we need."

"I'm going back to my hotel room," Bodie said.

"Why?"

"I've got some unfinished business," he said. "That's where I'll be if you need me."

"Very well," Fairburn said, knowing what Paul Bodie's unfinished business was like. "I'll send for you if I need you."

Clint sent a telegram to the U.S. Marshal's Office in Jefferson City, requesting a marshal be dispatched to Truxton as soon as possible to investigate the matter of a murder, and a false arrest. Normally, such a request would be made by a law enforcement official, but he hoped that—in this case—his name would make a difference.

When he got to the hotel Kate was there waiting for him.

"What happened with the doctor?" he asked.

"He's already at the jail. And the marshal?"

"No reply yet," Clint said. "I told the operator I'd be here."

"So now we just wait?"

Clint nodded.

"We wait for a judge," he said, "or a marshal, whichever comes first."

"Well," she said, "at least we know Wiley's alive."

"And we've got to keep him that way."

# THIRTY-SIX

Keeping Wilcox alive shouldn't be such a problem, Clint thought. For one thing nobody was going to be calling for his head, or trying to lynch him. Most of the homesteaders and businessmen would consider what he did—assuming he did it—a service to the community. So there was very little chance of anybody storming the jail.

Clint also figured there was very little chance of Wilcox being shot in the back while escaping. He didn't think Lake was the type.

He and Kate once again repaired to the hotel dining room to figure out what to do over coffee. He explained what he'd been thinking, and why he thought Wilcox would be safe while in custody.

"Now tell me something about Fairburn."

"Like what?"

"Is he powerful enough—no, is he rich enough to have a judge in his pocket?"

She thought only a moment before saying, "Yes, I think he is."

"Then we better hope that the federal marshal gets here first," Clint said.

"And what do we do when he gets here?"

"We'll have to prove that Wiley didn't kill Simon Butcher . . . you know, the window guy?"

"I know who he is."

Good, he thought, somebody finally remembers the poor dead man.

"How do we prove it?"

"I guess we'll have to find out who did it."

"How do we do that?" she asked. "I don't know the first thing about being a detective."

"We don't have to be detectives," he said, "we just have to ask questions."

"Who do we ask?"

"Well, we're pretty sure that Fairburn is behind the death of Butcher, and that means—more directly—that Bodie probably is."

"Paul," Kate said, "I can talk to him."

"No."

"But I know him."

"No."

"I can get him to—"

"Kate?"

"Yes?"

"That's not a good idea."

"Why not?"

"Consider your history with him."

She looked as if she was doing just that.

"Would you be able to stand up to him? Lie to him, convincingly?"

She thought about that for a moment.

"Probably not," she admitted. "I never could lie to him."

"So it's not a real good idea for you to be alone with him."

"No," she admitted, "it's not."

"In fact," Clint said, "maybe you shouldn't even be involved—"

"Oh, no," she said, "Wiley's my husband. I've got to do something to get him out of jail. Hey, maybe we can break him out."

"That would get him out of jail," Clint pointed out, "but it wouldn't set him free."

"You're right," she said. "We've got make sure he's cleared. God!"

"What?"

"I was just thinking," she said, "if he went to jail how could I divorce him?"

"You wouldn't have to."

"Why not?"

"If he's convicted of murder," Clint said, "they'll hang him."

# THIRTY-SEVEN

As they were leaving the hotel Clint had an idea.

"There were four men with Bly when he ambushed Butcher," Clint said.

"Do you know any of them?"

"Just one name," he said. "Sam."

"Then I guess we have to find Sam," she said. "How do we do that?"

"The hard way," Clint said. "We'll have to start looking . . . and walking."

They walked around town together, with Clint examining the faces of men as they walked by them. Kate couldn't help him because she didn't recognize "Sam" by his description.

"I haven't seen him," Clint said, after a few hours.

"Maybe we should do something more direct."

"Like what?"

"We could ask Walter Fairburn where this Sam is."

"I get the feeling that the only employee Fairburn has any contact with is Bodie," Clint said. "He said that if he was a rancher, Bodie would be his foreman."

"Okay, then," she said, "we could ask Paul."

"And why would he tell us how to find this fella, Sam?" Clint asked.

She hesitated, then said, "I don't know, I'm just throwing out ideas, here."

"Well," Clint said, "you may have a point, in a way."

"What do you mean, in a way?"

"We don't have to ask Bodie," Clint said, "we can just watch him."

"Without him seeing us?"

"It wouldn't be easy," Clint said, "because he knows both of us on sight."

"Then how do we do it?"

"Carefully," Clint said, "very carefully . . . but before we do that there's one other way."

"What's that?"

"The saloon, tonight," Clint said. "I'll go to the saloon tonight and see if I see him. If not, then we'll start following Bodie tomorrow."

"I'll come to the saloon, too."

"No, you won't," Clint said. "You'll attract too much attention. I'll do it alone."

"And what will I do?"

"You'll wait at the hotel."

"Just wait?"

"Just wait."

"Well . . . what can we do now?"

"Let's go and see the doctor. He can tell us how Wiley is."

"Good idea. His office is this way. . . ."

# THIRTY-EIGHT

The doctor's name was Van Gelder, and he had been living in Truxton for over twenty years.

"Came here from the East," the white-haired man said. His face was heavily lined, almost seamed, but he had very clear, blue eyes. Clint guessed he was in his sixties, but wouldn't have been surprised if he turned out to be in his eighties.

"How is Wiley, Doc?" Kate asked as soon as they entered the man's office.

"Some bumps and bruises," the physician said. "One bad cut on his face that I stitched. He'll have a scar, though."

"That won't bother Wiley," Kate said. "He's already got so many scars on his body."

"Did you have any trouble getting in to see him?" Clint asked. "The sheriff didn't try to stop you, did he?"

"Oh, no," Van Gelder said, "he wouldn't have

been able to, anyway. I don't know if you've noticed, but our sheriff is pretty weak-willed."

"How did he get to be sheriff?"

Van Gelder looked at Kate.

"He knows about Fairburn."

"There you go," Van Gelder said. "Fairburn's handpicked man . . . *because* he's weak-willed. Understand?"

"Perfectly, Doctor."

Clint knew about the politics of small towns. He had dealt with the same things when he was a deputy, and when he was a sheriff, years ago.

"Wiley will survive his injuries, Kate," Doc Van Gelder said. "I only hope he survives everything else."

"You don't think he killed anyone, do you, Doc?" she asked.

"No, my dear, I do not."

"Thanks, Doc."

Clint shook the doctor's hand and they left his office.

"Where to now?" she asked.

"The sheriff's office," Clint said. "I want to talk to Wiley again."

Lake didn't like it, but he let them in to talk to Wilcox again, relieving Clint of his gun and gun belt.

Wilcox had a bandage on his cheek, and his eyes looked brighter. He was sitting on the cot, not lying on it, and his shoulders were not quite as slumped as they had been earlier.

"You're looking better, Wiley," Clint said.

"Thanks, I feel a little better. Hello, Kate."

"Hi, Wiley."

"Why are you back?" Wilcox asked Clint.

"I wanted to see if you remembered anything else," Clint said.

"Just that somebody hit me," Wilcox said. "Son of a bitch must have been hiding behind the overturned buckboard."

"That's probably why they turned it over in the first place."

"That's what I think," Wilcox said. "They set the bait and I walked right into the trap."

"That's the way it seems."

"Wonder if I'll be able to walk out again."

"You've got to keep thinking, Wiley," Clint said. "Come up with something that will help us prove that you're innocent."

"I'll try," Wilcox said. "They pretty much kept me in the dark—I mean, really in the dark." He looked at Kate. "Are you okay?"

"I'm fine," she said. "Don't worry about me. Clint and I are going to prove you didn't kill anyone."

"Thanks."

"You're going to need a lawyer," Clint said. "Is there one in town?"

"One," Wilcox said.

"Do you want me to approach him—"

"It won't do any good."

"Why not?"

"Simms—the lawyer? He works for Walter Fairburn."

# THIRTY-NINE

"There's got to be another lawyer," Clint said, outside the jail.

"Not in town," Kate said.

"What about a nearby town?"

"Emma and Petrie are the closest ones," she said. "I don't know if they have a lawyer—but Jefferson City does. It has plenty of lawyers."

It would, Clint thought, being the state capital.

"Well," he said, "I wired for a federal marshal, I might as well wire for a lawyer."

Later that evening Clint and Kate were in the lobby of the hotel.

"I still think I should come," she said. "I could tuck my hair under my hat, and nobody would know I was a woman."

"And what are you going to do about your body?" he asked.

She looked down at herself, and then smiled at him.

"I don't know, what would you like me to do about it?" she asked.

"Keep it here, in the hotel, until I get back."

"You'll come to my room when you do?"

He nodded.

"To let you know I'm back."

"Of course," she said. "I didn't have anything else in mind."

Clint went to the White Branch Saloon first, because that was where he had had his altercation with Bly and Sam. If anyone would know where Sam was it would be someone there.

He decided to play it safe first and not ask for him. Instead he stood at the bar, nursing a beer, hoping Sam would come in on his own.

"Another one?" the bartender asked after he'd nursed the same beer for almost two hours.

"Yeah, sure."

The bartender brought him another, which he sipped. After drinking lukewarm beer for so long, the cold one felt good going down.

"Waiting for someone?" the bartender asked.

"Maybe."

"Who? Maybe I can help."

"I'll just wait awhile longer," Clint said. "Thanks for the offer."

Clint had a feeling Bly and Sam were regulars in the saloon. The bartender wouldn't be about to help a virtual stranger cause them trouble.

After another half hour Clint finally saw a familiar

face. It wasn't Sam, though. It was the dark-haired girl he'd met that night, Emily.

When she saw him she came up to him, flashing him a smile that almost took his mind off her cleavage.

"You came back," she said.

"Yes, I did."

"I was hoping you would," she said. "Would you like to go upstairs?"

"More than anything," he said, "I just wouldn't like to pay for it."

"A girl's gotta make a living," she said. "Can't do that givin' it away."

"I understand," he said. "A paying customer comes first."

"If you change your mind—"

"Maybe you can help me with something, Emily," he said, before she could walk away.

"Like what?"

"That first night I got here you were with two men."

"One man," she said. "Stacy was with the other."

"Which one were you with?"

"I was with Andy."

"That would be Bly."

"That's right," she said, then looked surprised, like she just remembered something. "He got killed. Were you the one—"

"I'm the one," Clint said. "He tried to kill me first. I had no other choice."

"You don't have to convince me," she said. "Him gettin' killed didn't surprise me at all."

"I'm looking for the other man, Sam?"

"Sam Dade," she said. "You gonna kill him, too?"

"I just want to ask him some questions."

"Well, he should be in here to see Stacy. He comes in every night. He's a regular paying customer."

"What time will he be in?"

"Should be within the hour. Want me to tell him you're lookin' for him?"

"No," Clint said, "if he knows, he might run."

"Well, when he comes in and goes upstairs, you'll need some help gettin' up there."

"I guess I will."

"But he might see you."

"He might."

"That is," she said coyly, "unless you go up with me now. That way, you'll already be there when he gets here."

"But how will I know he's here?"

"I'll check with Stacy and let you know."

"And what do you get out of this?" he asked.

"A paying customer?"

Clint thought a moment, then said, "Sure, why not?"

Even self-imposed rules were made to be broken, sometime.

# FORTY

Clint went upstairs with Emily and she showed him down the hall to her room.

"The sheets are new," she said, as she closed the door behind them. "I changed them before I came down."

"That's nice to know," he said. In fact, he could smell the newness of the sheets, so he knew she was telling him the truth.

She crossed the room and sat on the bed. The amount of flesh she was showing by crossing her legs and leaning forward was enticing.

"I have to collect the money first," she said. "House rule."

"Right. How much?"

She told him and he handed it over.

"Just to make you feel better," she said, walking to the dresser and putting the money in the top drawer, "this is not for sex, it's for giving you a chance to talk to Sam Dade."

"Right."

"Still," she said, turning to him and sliding her dress off her shoulders, "that doesn't mean that we can't spend the time getting acquainted."

Her plump breasts bobbed free as she slid the dress down and let it drop to the floor. She removed a silky undergarment and stood before him naked. The tangle of hair between her legs was as black as the hair on her head. Her breasts, though plump, were not especially large. Her nipples were dark brown, the aureola very large. Her skin was pale, contrasting the color of her nipples. They reminded Clint of chocolate pudding.

And she looked just as sweet. . . .

Later, Emily sat up, her body covered with a fine sheen of perspiration. She ran her hands down over Clint's belly to hold his semierect penis in her hand.

"You have a lot of stamina," she said. "Most of the men who come here are in and out and finished in minutes."

"Doesn't sound like much fun to me," he said, looking down at her hand as she rubbed him. He felt himself beginning to respond, his penis thickening and lengthening again.

"Even more stamina than I thought," she said, releasing him and eyeing him appreciatively.

"Don't you think you should check and see if Sam is visiting your friend?" he asked.

She leaned over and took him in both hands this time, gently, and said, "In a minute or two . . . or more . . ."

He felt her hot mouth come down on him, and

engulf him, and he had to lie back and close his eyes. She was very, very good at this. . . .

She got up later and slid on her dress without bothering with underwear.

"God," she said, tugging at the dress here and there until the fit was right, "my legs are weak."

"*Your* legs are weak?" he asked. "I don't know if I'll be able to walk down the hall."

"Well, you better get dressed before you try," she suggested. "While you're doing that I'll go down and check and see if he's there."

She left the room and he sat up in bed and started to dress. The things he had to do to help a friend. As he pulled on his boots, he thought about her chocolate pudding nipples. He'd been wrong about them being as sweet . . . they were even sweeter.

By the time she came back into the room he was dressed, on his feet, and wearing his gun.

"Is he there?"

"He's there," Emily said. "Give him a minute and he'll be . . . well, shall we say, vulnerable?"

# FORTY-ONE

Clint slipped out of Emily's room, telling her to stay there.

"I can stay right here," she said, pointing to the bed, "and wait for you to finish."

"I won't be able to come back," he said, then added, "not tonight."

"Oh, well," she said, "there's always tomorrow."

"Thanks, Emily," he said, "for everything."

"Thank you, too, Clint," she said, "for giving me a break from the usual selfish cowboys I entertain."

"Which room is hers?"

"Five," she said, "right down the hall."

"Thanks."

Now he moved down the hall to room five and quietly turned the doorknob. It wasn't locked, so he pushed the door open.

The naked girl in the bed was blond, with large, pear-shaped breasts that were not as solid as Emily's but had a certain charm of their own.

The naked man had no charm at all. He'd been pawing the breasts just before Clint entered the room, leaving red welts on the girl's skin.

When the man saw Clint, he started to reach for the gun on the bedpost.

"Don't," Clint said. "You'll never make it."

The man froze.

"Stacy, why don't you get dressed and wait outside?"

She didn't need to be told twice. She scrambled away from the man, pulled on her dress, and left.

"What is this?"

"Recognize me, Sam?"

"Sure," Sam said. "You killed Bly."

"Who told you that?" Clint asked. "You were with him here that first night, but who told you I killed him?"

"I heard. Can I get dressed?"

"No," Clint said, "I think I like you this way."

"You like lookin' at naked men?"

"No, I just think you're too embarrassed to try something while you're naked. I tell you what, though. Sit up in the bed with the sheet over you, if you're that modest."

Sam did just that. He got into the bed, pulled the sheet over him, and sat with his back against the bedpost.

"Now, you can answer my questions, or your gun is on the bedpost. You can go for it any time you feel lucky."

Sam scowled.

"What kind of questions?"

"I want to know where Paul Bodie was holding Wiley Wilcox until this morning. That's one."

"What's two?" Sam asked. "Maybe that one won't get me killed."

"You were one of the men shooting at the homestead inspector that first day, weren't you?"

"Yeah, I was."

"And Bly?"

"Yeah."

"What were you trying to do?"

"Whataya think we were trying to do?"

"Kill him?"

Sam hesitated, then said, "Yeah."

"But I got in the way."

"Yeah, you did."

"What about yesterday?"

"What about it?"

"I wasn't in the way, then," Clint said. "You killed him yesterday, then waited for Wilcox to come along. You knocked him out, then held him someplace until this morning, to make him look guilty."

"I was in on all that, except killing him. I came along after he was dead."

"So who killed him?"

"I don't know."

"Who do you think killed him?"

Sam's eyes flicked toward his gun.

"It's too late for that, Sam," Clint said. "You've answered most of the questions. Why get killed for holding out on one or two more?"

Sam hesitated, then made a face and said, "Yeah, you're right. It's time to leave this town . . . I can leave, can't I? After this?"

"Sure," Clint said, "you can leave. Just tell me who you think killed him."

"It was Bodie, I think."

"And then you and somebody else waited to ambush Wilcox, right?"

"Right."

"And where was he kept?"

"There's a cabin a few miles outside of town. It's got a root cellar."

"Give me better directions to this cabin."

Sam did, and Clint committed them to memory.

"Now tell me, would you testify in court?"

Sam shook his head.

"You might as well kill me now,'cause that would get me killed for sure. Besides, I didn't see Bodie do it, you know."

"I thought you might say that."

"Look, can I go now? I got to pack a few things and get my horse."

"Sure, Sam," Clint said. "Leave town. If I see you here tomorrow, you'll wish you had left. Understand?"

"I'm leaving, Adams," Sam said. "Now, if you get outta here I can get dressed."

"I'm going," Clint said. "Don't make any mistakes, Sam."

"I'm not lookin' to die," Sam said, "and I was never lookin' to tangle with you."

"Good," Clint said. "Stay that smart, and stay alive."

Clint backed out the door and into the hall, where Stacy was waiting.

"Stacy, I'd go downstairs and look for another customer, if I were you."

"Do I have to give him his money back?"

"I don't think he's going to be worried about it."

"How about you?" she asked, smiling. "Seeing

as how I'm already paid for. We can use Emily's room. In fact, maybe Emily and I could—"

"As enticing as that sounds, Stacy, I can't. I just don't have the time."

Stacy made a face and said, "Too bad."

Yeah, Clint thought as he walked down the hall to the stairs, it is.

# FORTY-TWO

When Clint got back to the hotel Kate was waiting up for him. He knocked on the door one time and she flung it open.

"Where've you been?" she asked, and immediately—illogically—Clint felt like an errant husband.

"Uh, well, it took a while."

"Did you get the information we needed?"

"Yes."

"You found him?"

"Yes."

"Where is he?"

"By now he should be out of town."

"You let him go?"

"Yes, Kate," Clint said, "I let him go after he gave me what I needed."

"Well, come inside and tell me—" she started to say, but as she stepped into the hall to touch his arm she stiffened. Clint could see her sniffing the air, and knew that she smelled the other woman on him.

She backed into the room again.

"I'm kind of tired, Kate," he said. "We can talk in the morning."

"Sure," she said, "I understand. You're tired. Why wouldn't you be? You got *everything* you needed tonight, didn't you?"

"Kate—"

"Never mind," she said, holding her hand up to stop him. "You don't have to account to me, Clint. I mean, it's not like we're married or anything."

"Kate, listen—"

"Good night," she said. "Just say good night and I'll see you in the morning."

"Good—" he started to say, but she slammed the door in his face.

Lately it seemed like he was running into demanding women who wanted sex, and he was getting into trouble for giving it to them. Maybe, he thought, he should just practice keeping his pants closed. Maybe he'd get in less trouble that way.

He started down the hall to his room.

Kate was right about one thing. There was no need for him to explain, or feel guilty, because they weren't married. Hell, they weren't even friends, really. She was his friend's wife. He didn't owe her an explanation for going to bed with another woman.

As he opened the door to his room and stepped inside, he wondered why he *still* felt like a cheating husband who'd been caught.

# FORTY-THREE

In the morning the tension was still there. Clint could feel it in the building, even before he walked down the hall to knock on her door. Unlike the morning before, she was dressed and ready.

"Let's get some breakfast," he said.

"I'm not really hungry."

"Well, I am," Clint said. "I don't operate well on an empty stomach."

"I'll have coffee."

They went to the dining room and Clint ordered his breakfast. Kate made a production out of drinking a cup of coffee.

"Kate, we should talk—"

"Not about last night," she said calmly. "There's nothing to talk about. I don't have any claim on you, and I don't want an explanation."

"Okay, fine," he said. "I'll just tell you what I learned from Sam."

"Fine."

Briefly he related the conversation he had had with Sam, leaving out the part about him being naked with a whore. At least he didn't have to explain how he *had* to have sex with a whore while he was waiting to catch Sam with his pants down.

"So, what will finding the place where they held Wiley prove?" she asked.

"I don't know," Clint said. "Maybe we'll find something there, maybe not."

"And what about this Sam?" she asked. "You told me last night he was leaving town."

"Yes, I did," Clint said, "but I know where he's going, and he'll come back to testify against Fairburn and Paul Bodie."

"He will? That's great."

Clint studied her face for a few moments, until she became uncomfortable.

"Clint, will you excuse me?"

"Is something wrong?"

"I just forgot something upstairs," she said. "I'll be right back."

"Sure, Kate," he said. "I have to eat my breakfast anyway."

She stood up and left the dining room. Clint watched her until she was out the door. If he'd moved his chair a bit he would have been able to see if she went upstairs, or out the door, but he didn't bother. He hoped she would do one, but he was prepared if she did the other.

Clint was halfway finished with his breakfast by the time Kate returned. He didn't bother asking what she had forgotten. He didn't want to sit there and try to figure out if she was lying or not.

"All set?" he asked.

"Yes," she said, "fine."

He finished his breakfast and they left to walk to the livery.

"You have no problem with me going with you?" she asked.

"No."

"Why not?"

"Because it'll be just you and me," he said, "won't it?"

"Well, yes."

"Last night you would have attracted too much attention," he said. "Today's a different story."

As they approached the livery he asked, "Do you have a gun?"

"No."

From inside his shirt he produced the little Colt New Line he sometimes carried as a hide-out gun.

"Here. It's small, but it will do the job."

She took it and looked at it.

"Just tuck it into your belt," he said. "Do you know how to use it?"

"Yes," Kate said, tucking it away. "I've fired a gun before."

"Good. I don't expect that you'll need it, but it's better to be safe."

"I agree."

When they got to the livery they saddled their own horses and walked them outside.

"You have the directions on how to get there?" she asked.

"Yes," he said, "very precise directions. It won't be hard to find."

"I still don't know what you expect to find there," she commented.

"I don't expect to find anything," Clint said. "Let's just see what happens when we get there."

They mounted up and rode out of town. Trying not to let her notice, Clint started to inch Duke back so that Kate had the lead. She didn't notice, either, but they were still going in the right direction, which was all the proof Clint needed that the thought that had occurred to him during the night was the right one.

Kate Wilcox was not at all what she seemed, or claimed to be.

# FORTY-FOUR

The house was small, in disrepair but still standing. The land around it was overgrown, and there was a broken-down corral nearby. Obviously, someone had once lived there, tried to make a go of it, and failed. Maybe they'd been taxed for too many windows.

They rode up to the house and dismounted. Clint dropped Duke's reins to the ground, knowing that he wasn't going anywhere. Kate tied her horse off to a half fallen hitching post.

"Where do we start?" she asked.

"Inside," Clint said. "There's supposed to be a root cellar."

"Well, the door to it might be outside."

"Okay," he said, "you look outside and I'll look inside. Sing out if you find something."

"Okay."

He went into the small house. It was all one room. The windows had long since lost their glass. Off to one side there was what used to be a kitchen. There were pieces of wood strewn about that used to be furniture of some kind. He looked for a trapdoor on the floor that would lead to a root cellar, but there was none. That was okay. He hadn't expected to find it anyway. He was sure the door would be outside the building. He just wanted to give Kate a chance to do what she was going to do.

If she could.

He could see her shadow streaming in the window behind him. It blended with his, but he was still able to make out that her arm was raised, no doubt holding the gun he had given her. He gave her ample time to pull the trigger, and then turned when she didn't.

"Can't do it, Kate?"

She stared at him.

"I should," she said, glaring at him, "after what you did last night with that whore when you could have had me."

"Is that what this is about?" he asked. "I spurned you? Cheated on you?"

"I gave myself to you, you son of a bitch. It could have been Bodie—"

"Stop, Kate," Clint said. "I know you were in on this from the beginning."

"In on what?" she asked. "What do you think you know?"

"Well, I don't *know* anything, really," Clint said. "I do, however, *think* a few things."

"Like what?"

"Like I said, you were in on it from the beginning, with Paul Bodie."

"I told you I wasn't with Bodie—"

"You also told me you hadn't cheated on your husband with him, or anyone else, until me, but the woman I was with that night wouldn't—couldn't—go without sex for two years. You have too much appetite for it, Kate. So that was a lie."

She didn't answer, just continued to train the New Line on him through the window.

"Now this is what I think," Clint said. "I think a man like Walter Fairburn buys a lot of land, and I think he wanted Wiley's land, only Wiley wouldn't sell. For some reason, he wouldn't sell to Fairburn—at least, not when Fairburn made his offer."

No reply from Kate.

"I'll bet if Fairburn had waited, say, two weeks, and made an offer, Wiley would have taken it."

"Wiley wouldn't sell to Fairburn," Kate said. "Not at any price. To someone else, yeah, but not to Fairburn."

"So there it is," Clint said. "The only way for Fairburn to get Wiley's land, and keep him from selling it to someone else, was to frame him for murder—and who better for a victim than the window man? Everybody hated the window man, right?"

No answer.

"And you helped, didn't you? I'll bet you told Bodie exactly when Butcher would be out at your ranch. Or maybe Bodie was nearby, waiting and watching. Wiley went for his ride and you signaled Bodie, or one of his men. I think Bodie did the actual killing—that's what Sam said, anyway. Then he had a couple of his men waylay Wiley and take him here, put him in the root cellar. Where's the door, Kate? Right out there by your feet?"

Her eyes flicked down for only a second, but that was his answer.

"You were up early this morning, weren't you?

Went out to see Bodie? Wanted to find out what you should do?''

No answer.

''Then when you left me in the dining room you went to him and told him about Sam testifying, and about us coming out here. He should be along pretty soon, shouldn't he?''

''He'll be here.''

''Because you told him about Sam, right? And he wants to know where Sam is?''

''You'll tell him.''

She flexed her hand. Holding the gun was starting to be a chore.

''No, I won't.''

''Why not?''

''Because I don't know.''

''But you said—''

''I lied.''

''What?''

''I don't know where Sam went, only that he left town,'' Clint explained. ''He said he wouldn't testify, so I let him go.''

''But . . .''

''But now Bodie's on his way out here, and you've given yourself away, like I figured you would.''

She frowned, as if trying to figure this all out.

''You knew?''

''I suspected, Kate,'' he said. ''I hoped I was wrong—because I like you—but I suspected . . . *strongly* suspected that I wasn't.''

''You son of a bitch,'' she said. ''You lied to me.''

''Why not? You lied to me.''

''Not about that night, I didn't,'' she said. ''Not about wanting you. I would have turned on Bodie for you, but you'd rather be with some whore.''

"We're back to that, are we? You're a woman scorned?''

"I should kill you now,'' she said.

"You had your chance, Kate,'' he said. "If you were going to do it, you would have by now.''

She firmed her pretty jaw and flexed her hand.

"Give me the gun.''

He started for the window.

"Don't.''

He kept coming.

"Clint!''

He didn't stop.

"Damn you and your whore!'' she said viciously and pulled the trigger.

# FORTY-FIVE

Paul Bodie reined his horse in when he came within sight of the house. He'd been surprised when Kate Wilcox came to him that morning. She'd gotten him out of bed with the young and willing Hazel to tell him about Clint Adams and Sam Dade. . . .

"Why are you telling me this, Kate?" Bodie asked. "I thought you were through with me after that window fella."

"I didn't agree with you killing him and framing Wiley," she said.

"And you're helping Adams try to prove I framed him to get back at me," Bodie said, "I know."

"Not anymore."

Bodie closed the door of his room and stepped into the hall. He was wearing a pair of trousers he'd hastily pulled on, and nothing else.

"What happened?" he asked. "Trouble in paradise?"

"Do you want my help or not?"

"I've seen that look before," he said, ignoring her question. "That time you found me in bed with that young—"

"Forget it!"

"Okay, wait, wait," Bodie said. "Yes, I want your help. What's going on?"

And she told him about Sam Dade's willingness to testify, and about her and Adams coming out to the house where they'd kept Wilcox prisoner.

"I don't know what he hopes to find," she said.

"There is nothing for him to find," Bodie said, "but I want him out there. I'll have to get him to tell me where Sam is before I kill him."

He'd watched her face carefully.

"Do you mind if I kill him?"

"Do what you want," she said. "Kill him . . . unless I kill him first."

Now, looking down at the house from a rise, two horses out in front of it, Bodie hoped that Kate had not killed Clint Adams—not yet. He remembered her temper, though, when being scorned—not that he had ever scorned her for long. He always came back to her—until the day she left, of course. But he always managed to find her, and they always managed to end up together—one way or another.

She was so unhappy in her marriage that she had offered to help Bodie get Wiley Wilcox's land for Walter Fairburn. As it turned out, though, she was not all that much help. Her influence over her husband was minimal, at best. She couldn't talk him into selling, so she'd agreed to help another way.

Bodie felt that she knew what he was going to do,

kill the window man and frame Wilcox, but she pretended she didn't. He'd always been able to read Kate fairly well, but the way she reacted to Clint Adams had puzzled him.

Apparently, Adams had not responded in kind, and so here they all were.

Alive and well.

He hoped.

''What if he doesn't come?''

Clint turned away from the window and looked at Kate, huddled in a corner. The gun he'd given her had clicked on the empty shells he'd loaded the gun with. He'd taken the gun from her and hauled her into the house right over the window ledge. He'd spent some time during the night prying the lead off the bullets and emptying the powder out, then replacing the lead, effectively loading the gun with blanks.

He hadn't really expected her to pull the trigger, but in the end she had. He was glad he'd decided to play it safe.

''You pulled the trigger,'' he had said. ''That disappoints me, Kate.''

''You lied to me again!'' she said. ''The gun wasn't loaded.''

''It's loaded with blanks,'' he said. He was holding her by the arm he'd grabbed to pull her in.

''You're hurting me.''

''You just tried to kill me.''

''You rejected me,'' she said, ''but that wasn't enough. You had to humiliate me, as well. You're like all the rest. I've never met a man I could trust.''

He pushed her away from him and said, ''Sit in

that corner while we wait for your boyfriend to show up."

"He's not my boyfriend," she said, sliding down in the corner, "but while I could never trust him, either, I could always count on him."

"That's what I'm doing," Clint said. "Counting on him to show up."

"Are we going down, boss?" one of the two men he'd brought with him asked.

"Yes," he said, "we're going down, but this is the way we'll do it . . ."

# FORTY-SIX

"Here he comes," Clint said.

"Alone?"

Without looking at her he said, "He wants me to think he is."

Now he turned and looked at her.

"What's he think we're doing here?"

"Looking around, I guess."

"Nothing else?"

She gave him a look and said, "I can't help what he thinks."

"He's riding right up here easy as you please," Clint said. "He can't really think I believe he's alone."

"I told you, he has a lot of confidence."

"Maybe he does," Clint said, "but he's not a fool."

Paul Bodie was almost up to the house when Clint shouted, "That's far enough, Bodie!"

Bodie reined his horse in.

‘‘Adams? Is that you?’’

‘‘It’s me.’’

‘‘You’re still alive.’’

‘‘Why wouldn’t I be?’’

‘‘The lady doesn’t like to be rejected,’’ Bodie said. ‘‘It makes her do crazy things sometimes. She can’t have changed that much.’’

‘‘She hasn’t,’’ Clint said. ‘‘She tried to shoot me.’’

‘‘Well, I’m glad she missed.’’

‘‘Why’s that, Bodie?’’

‘‘We need to talk.’’

‘‘About what?’’

‘‘Sam Dade.’’

‘‘What about him?’’

‘‘I need to know where he is.’’

‘‘I haven’t got a clue.’’

‘‘Kate said you did.’’

‘‘I lied to Kate.’’

He watched as Bodie digested that, tried to decide if it was true.

‘‘You son of a gun, you did, didn’t you?’’ Bodie’s tone was one of admiration.

‘‘Yes, I did.’’

‘‘That was good, Adams,’’ Bodie said, ‘‘I’m impressed. You got me out here.’’

‘‘And what do I do with that?’’ Clint asked. ‘‘Are you going to confess to killing Butcher and framing Wilcox so your boss could get his land?’’

‘‘Why would I do that?’’

‘‘I don’t know,’’ Clint said. ‘‘I thought maybe you’d decide to be helpful.’’

‘‘No,’’ Bodie said, ‘‘I think I’ll just turn my horse around and ride back to town. You can’t prove a thing.’’

"Maybe not, but I can't let you go."

"Why not?"

"Because you didn't come alone," Clint said. "You'll ride away and the minute I step outside your men will gun me down. How many did you bring? Two? Four? No, I think you'd bring two. You're confident, but not overconfident, and yet you wouldn't want to overdo it—like sending five men after Butcher."

"That was Bly, the idiot," Bodie said. "I told him and Sam to do it, and he had to bring in some friends. They don't even work for me."

"So two, then. Am I right?"

"Why don't you step out here and find out, Adams?"

"Why don't I just shoot you where you sit?" Clint replied.

Bodie shook his head.

"Not your style."

Clint turned to Kate.

"You want to die?"

"You wouldn't—" She looked alarmed.

"Maybe not, but when lead starts flying you're likely to get hit."

"What do you want me to do?"

"Go look out the other windows, without being seen, and tell me what *you* see."

She got to her feet, but crouched over and moved to the other windows. There were three.

"I see two men," she said, returning to her corner. "One around back, one on the right side—our right side."

"The one around back might go around the left side, or try to come through the back window. Is there something around you can use as a club?''

She looked around and came up with something that looked like the leg of an old table.

''Yes.''

''Stand by the back window. If he sticks his head in, let him have it.''

''What if he comes around the side of the house?''

''At least I know where they are,'' Clint said.

''Are you stepping outside?''

''To finish this, yes.''

''You can't! They'll kill you.''

''Just stand by the back window and be ready, Kate.''

''Shoot him from here, Clint!''

''I can't.''

''Why not?''

''Like he says,'' Clint said, heading for the door, ''it's not my style.''

When he got to the door he stopped.

''Bodie!''

''I hear you!''

''I'm coming out!''

''Come ahead!''

Clint opened the door slowly and stepped out.

# FORTY-SEVEN

Clint stepped outside and saw Bodie, still on his horse.

"You want to get down," he asked, "or do it from there?"

"I think I'll do it from here," Bodie said. "Step farther out."

"I can see you from here."

Clint was only about a step or two out the door. This way he could use the house as cover from the other two. They'd have to step out themselves to get a decent shot at him.

"Well, go ahead," Clint said. "Let's do it."

"This doesn't get Wilcox off, you know," Bodie said. "Live or die, you can't prove he's innocent."

"I'll prove it," Clint said. "Kate will testify."

"You think so?"

"I know so."

"After you're dead?"

"After you are."

"You have a lot of confidence for a man who's outnumbered three to one," Bodie said.

At that moment Clint heard a sound from inside the house, like wood hitting flesh, and then a groan.

"Try two to one," he said.

Bodie went for his gun, angling his horse to use it as cover. At the same time a man stepped out from Clint's right.

The other man misjudged Clint's distance from the house. That meant he had to take another two steps, and that cost him his life.

Clint shot Bodie first. Angle or no, the shot hit him solid and took him from the saddle.

Clint turned quickly as the other man was taking his second step and killed him before he could complete it.

He turned again and saw Bodie struggling to his knees. He fired a third time, and the man keeled over on his back, dead. Kate's horse reeled from the sound of the shots, eyes wild, but when the shooting stopped he calmed down.

"Kate?"

She came to the door, still holding the chair leg.

"I got him," she said. "He stuck his head in the window, just like you said."

"Did you kill him?"

"I don't think so."

"Good, maybe he'll talk."

"I might as well talk, too," she said. "It'll get Wiley off."

"He'll appreciate it. Stay here, I'm just going to make sure they're dead."

# FORTY-EIGHT

Two days later Clint stepped from the hotel and found Wiley Wilcox waiting for him.

"You're out."

"Thanks to you," Wilcox said.

"And the federal marshal," Clint said. "Don't forget him."

"Sure, him, too."

"And Kate," Clint said. "What she told the marshal helped him make up his mind."

"She's gone, you know."

"I know," Clint said. "She left yesterday. You're looking good."

The cut on his face had scabbed over, and he'd removed the bandage.

"You leavin' today?"

"Yep."

"Walk you to the livery?"

"Sure."

As they walked Wilcox said, "I'll be leaving just

as soon as the sale of my place is final.''

''Who'd you decide to sell it to?''

Wilcox laughed without humor.

''You won't believe it.''

''Fairburn?''

Wilcox nodded.

''They couldn't prove nothin' against him,'' Wilcox said. ''Only Bodie.''

''Why sell it to him?''

''Why not?'' Wilcox asked. ''I want out, and that's the fastest way.''

''Kate said you'd never sell to him.''

''She never did know me well.''

''How are you going to work the divorce?''

''She's goin' to San Francisco,'' Wilcox said. ''I'll let her know where to send the papers for me. I'll sign 'em as soon as I get them.''

When they got to the livery Clint saddled Duke and walked him out.

''Got a good horse?'' Clint asked.

''I picked one out for myself,'' Wilcox said. ''I'll sell the rest. I tell you, the trail is going to be nice after a prison sentence.''

Clint mounted Duke and looked down at his friend, extending his hand.

''You weren't in jail that long,'' he said, as they shook hands.

Wilcox smiled and said, ''I wasn't talking about jail.''